JESUS

HEALS

THE BROKENHEARTED

with what David left behind

Mária Vágó Steers

To

Leann, David's wife

and

their children

Christalyn, Benjamin and Solomon

ACKNOWLEDGEMENTS

This book came about by a miracle of God.

I have never written a book in my life and never expected to write one. But through his tragic death our son David left behind for our family such a rich example of intimacy with God, that it had to be preserved in writing.

My husband did the major part by helping me with cherished memories, by faithfully critiquing what I have written, by enriching me with heartfelt suggestions and by doing much of the computer work. Our children, their families by marriage, many of our friends read the manuscript and added insightful and honest comments to make what had been written into a possible publication. Some came to our help with their computer expertise.

Then at our last visit to our son Philip in Saudi Arabia, at Christmas 2002, the Lord brought to him a professional journalist, Sue Willis and a professional Graphic Designer from Sri Lanka, Mike Fernando. They worked with me at our son's house to put the final touches on the book to make it ready for publication.

All of us have it in our hearts to make this writing a love-offering to our God.

Through His beloved Son, Jesus Christ, the heavenly Father has given us the privilege and authority to tell all people everywhere what He has done for us, so that they too will believe and obey Him, bringing glory to His name.

It is my prayer that through the message of this book all the readers will also hear God's invitation to them to become members of His family by faith in His beloved Son.

Maria Vágó Steers

CONTENTS

PREFACE

How is your faith when the unthinkable happens to you?

Such an event occurred in the lives of the Steers family on June 19, 1998. They received word that Phil and Maria's 40-year-old son, David, had died unexpectedly. He was the father of two children and with his wife they were expecting a third child with joyful anticipation. During and after the shock, the family experienced that faith in God's Word is truly the shield that quenches the devil's fiery darts of mistrust toward God. They were renewed in God instead of being crushed by the trauma.

Now David's mother, Maria Steers, has written this deeply felt account of how God, through His Word, triumphed in their hearts overcoming their shock and grief. All along He kept reassuring them that He will never change His love and kindness and tender mercies toward them. Not only their whole family, but their churches and friends also came together in a beautiful demonstration of how God is glorified in His people. As they kept holding on to God's promises He united their hearts to stand together in His love. Through this oneness in God they experienced together the victory that overcomes all the trials of this life. This account shows how God uses the circumstances of our lives to make Himself known more fully to our needy hearts.

We, who stood on the sidelines, fortifying the family with our prayers, give thanks to our heavenly Father because He is the God who answers prayers when we approach Him in the name of His beloved Son, our Lord Jesus Christ. His Word promises that He will abundantly grant enabling grace to those whom we uphold with our prayers. This joyful news will spread to many and cause thanksgiving to abound to the glory of God. 2 Corinthians 1:11, 4:15

We are sure that this book will be a blessing and encouragement to all who will read it.

Elmer and Millie Blaine
Manchester, CA

How This Book Was Born

by Prayer, a Rosebush And Many Tears

My husband and I were in tears, praying together.

The Lord had unexpectedly taken our 40-year-old son, David, to Himself. When it was my turn to pray, I kept thanking God for "what David left behind."

Phil interrupted me, "What David left behind blessed us so much! I wish you would write it down!"

Later on that day I passed our neighbor's house. He was out in front watering his rosebush. "What happened to your rosebush?" I called over to him in amazement, "Only a few days ago it seemed dead, and you chopped it down, but now it's full of the most beautiful, sparkling-red roses! Did you buy a new bush?"

No, this is the same bush," our neighbor answered. "After I chopped it down I just kept watering it, and God performed a miracle!"

In my heart I could hear God saying to me, "This is what I plan for your son David: You water "what David left behind," and I will make it blossom out, spreading My good news of unimaginable joy."

It is this promise from God that prompts me to write this book to the pleasure and glory of our God!

By faith in our Lord Jesus Christ,

David's mother,
Mária Vágó Steers

" The Smile He Left Behind"

David Dwight Steers

January 9, 1958 - June 19, 1998

This is how we last saw him.
We had a family picnic after Elise's wedding.

In his Bible David wrote:

*"We can have great joy in Jesus and
we can bring that joy to others."*

1993

David and Leann with their children
The loving father holds Benjamin and the hand of Christalyn

"The children are beloved of God for the sake of the father"
Romans 11; 28b

"The glory of the children is their father...."
Proverbs 17: 6b

1

THE NEWS THAT BROKE OUR HEARTS

Friday evening, June 19, 1998

After a pleasant dinner with Phil's sister and husband, Phil and I return home. A message waits for us on the phone answering machine:

"Mom and Dad Steers! David died this evening." It is the faint voice of Leann, our daughter-in-law. This is all she said.

Did we hear right? Is this possible? We must listen again! "David died!" The words crash into our hearts like a giant earthquake, threatening to wipe us off our feet.

David dead? With trembling fingers Phil dials Leann. No answer!

David! Our handsome, 40 year-old son is in excellent health—so full of life! David had just been transferred from Memphis, Tennessee, to Ridgeland, Mississippi, a suburb of Jackson, with a promotion and a raise. This August he and Leann would celebrate their twelfth wedding anniversary, and by then they would be enjoying the birth of their third child.

It is just two weeks ago that we had an unforgettable family celebration in Michigan at the wedding of Elise, our first grand-daughter. It is an unusual pleasure for our dispersed family to be together at once. The bride's parents, our son Philip and his wife Bonnie live in Saudi Arabia; our two daughters Yolan and Marion are married and live in Georgia; David and Leann just moved to Mississippi; Phil and I are retired in San Antonio, TX. It was a happy family reunion. David and Leann watched with delight as their children enjoyed their uncles, aunts, cousins and the new rela-tives. On all the photos David's joyful smile is very noticeable. Oh, that precious smile that David left behind!

"David died!" Our first thought of anguish is toward his chil-dren whom he leaves behind, his ten-year-old Christalyn, five-year-old Benjamin and Baby Solomon Isaac, expected to be born in about three weeks. How will this loss affect dear Leann, their mother? David so lovingly shared with her his devotion toward their children and his gratitude to God for another little boy soon to arrive in the family.

Phil phones our other children. "David died this evening." That is all we know for now. The shockwaves jolt through the family. We will never be the same!

We must go to Leann! We must find out what happened! We must go to help! Leann and the children need our love and compassion.

Immediately we start to pack. Hurriedly we throw our things into bags. By now it is close to midnight. We must try to get a little rest. Our drive will take at least ten hours non-stop from San Antonio to Ridgeland. We toss and turn but cannot sleep.

I keep calling out to God in despair: "Dear Lord Jesus, help us!"

Saturday, June 20, 1998, 4:00 AM

We gather our bags to head toward the door. But wait! There are important letters I must be sure to take with me. On the dining room table there is a Father's Day card from David. It just came yesterday morning. We had placed it on the dining room table with other cards from our children. We always enjoy reading them over and over.

Tomorrow is Sunday, Father's Day!

Can it be possible that David is gone? His card had arrived just hours before the heartbreaking news! Can this card really be the last token of love that he left behind for his dad? We will read it again in the car.

There is another message from David that I must take with me. It is in a large white envelope. He handed it to me at Elise's wedding. He wrote it by hand with the paragraphs in different colors. As David handed it to me Leann remarked, "Be sure to notice the different colors. They call to your attention that what David wrote is very important to him and to me. He made me listen to the letter as he read it out loud. He showed me how he arranged the colors."

Oh! We will be crushed having to read that letter now! Could it really be his last message to us? It has become David's 'last will' left behind for us!

His letter's purpose is to help us understand why he and Leann had determined to have their expected Baby Solomon to be baptized. Their decision is new to Phil and me because we did not practice infant baptism for our children. When our babies were born, we dedicated them to God in church. They were baptized later, when they were old enough to make it their own decision. Our other children followed that same custom. David left us a solemn message.

Like a dagger the thought cuts into my heart. "Baby Solomon's daddy will never hold his little boy in his arms."

It's still dark as we set off on our long drive. We unceasingly offer up to God our tearful, heartbroken prayers. Phil keeps his eye on the road with much effort.

As soon as there is a little light, I reach for the Father's Day card from David. On the background there are footprints in the sand. David liked to walk around barefoot, remembering his childhood in the tropics of Panama. He was born and reared there while his dad worked for the Panama Canal Company. I try to read the card to Phil but can't. Tears choke off my voice. It takes time before I am able to form this message into words:

Father's Day Card

Our tears flow, both Phil's and mine. What precious words remain behind from David for his dad! These priceless words tear at our hearts, "Thanks for being the Dad you are!" David left behind a treasure for his dad. Any comment that we could have made is choked off by the sound of our brokenhearted weeping.

"David is dead. What is God doing with us?" I wonder in deep confusion. "What is God doing to our family? How can we face this sudden, tragic death? What happened to David?" Urgent prayers keep welling up within me:

> Our Lord God, why was our son's life cut short before he could raise his children? He loved his family so very much. Why did You turn David and Leann's joyful expectation of their baby into a tragedy? Why was this father's life taken from him before he could get to see his baby?

Further mental anguish tortures me. How will the news of this tragedy affect our extended family and friends in Europe, in Saudi Arabia and in South America? Some of them are not believers. We have purposely made visits to them in order to share with them our faith in the Lord Jesus and our assurance that because of Him our family is blessed in a special way.

Phil and I are filled with troubling questions. How can this tragic blow, this sudden loss of our precious son, count as a blessing from God? Did God forget that David has a wife and children and that the third child is to be born shortly? How can we believe this as a blessing? How can we explain this to anyone as God's continued goodness toward our family? This puzzle is tearing at our hearts.

Behind the clouds the sun is beginning to rise, painting shining gold edges around them. Then the warm, radiant beams send glowing rays downward from heaven to earth.

"Look," Phil remarks. "I take these shining rays from on high as rays of hope. Look at them! God is assuring us that in the midst of our grief His purpose is to shower us with His grace. God promises to work His goodness into every circumstance of our lives."

But I am still troubled. I ponder a memory that I had cherished with our grandchildren. They had called me outside to join them in admiring a beautiful rainbow in the sky. The magnificent sight caused me to exclaim, "The rainbow is God's message that He will always be kind to us!" One of our little grandsons was so happy to hear this that he burst out, "Oh, grandma, say that again!"

Can I still say to our grandchildren that God is always kind when He has taken their Uncle David from them? Can I say to Christalyn and Benjamin that God is kind when He has torn their daddy from them? And can I say to Baby Solomon that God is kind when he will never see his daddy in this life? God's promise seems like a contradiction now.

I am accustomed to keeping a daily diary of what God is saying to me in the mornings from my Bible reading. I wonder, "What did I write in it yesterday morning? How did God prepare me for what I had to face that day?" I take out my diary from my purse and curiously turn to my notations from the past days to refresh my memory. Then I read what I wrote yesterday morning:

Friday morning, June 19, 1998

An overwhelming, evil terror startled me out of bed in the dark at 4:00 AM. I am overcome by what the powers of darkness are doing in America. It seems that the biblical family is the main target of attack. The evil powers have taken over the rule in America! An evil, satanic opposition to the work of God is prevailing in our nation. Who can stop this?

I had fallen on my knees crushed with despair for our children and grandchildren who are surrounded with the present sin-loving culture of America. There is no longer any shame over disobedience toward God as there had been in our nation's past. Even in our own family one couple has been under powerful evil attack and on the verge of breaking up. They are both Christians, but one of them is drifting from God.

Rebellion against God's law is in the daily news. It is invading our homes, our schools, our media, our movies, even the White House and, worst of all, our churches. The Supreme Court and our Congress legislate sin as "constitutional," while God's Word, the Ten Commandments, the name of Jesus and prayers are legislated as "unconstitutional" and "un-American" in our public life.

Even Christians are trapped by the devil to believe his lie, "You have time! You have time to seek your own fun and play, to join the unbelievers in their amusements." When all is well, it is easy to ignore Jesus' warning:

> *"Watch therefore,*
> *For you do not know at what hour your Lord is coming . . .*
> *Therefore you also be ready, for the Son of man is coming at an hour you do not expect." Mathew 24:42,44 NKJ*
>
> *"Watch therefore, and pray always." Luke 21:36a NKJ*

In my diary I closed my notes with the promises of Jesus. I would cling to these:

I send the promise of My Father upon you. You will be endued with power from on high to stand successfully, with the whole armor of God, against the evil powers .
I will build My church, My family . . .You are My family.

At the end I added in large letters:

JESUS IS VICTOR!
Stand on the final outcome!

"You are My family! I will build My family!" I must hold on to these reassuring words. So then, even in the midst of this painful trial, Jesus' purpose for our family is to be built up. All around us families are falling apart. Jesus has a mighty purpose in our family. Jesus will use our family, in some unforeseen way, to rebuild many other families and to build love and unity into His own family, the Church.

My morning time with God yesterday was so startling that I needed to share my impressions with someone. My first thought was of Leann. With the day of her baby's arrival so near, she would need special encouragement. It would help her to know how God strengthened me at the time when my babies were born. I sat down to write a letter to her and spent most of the day writing. I brought this letter, also, with me in my purse. While I was writing it, I had no idea that on the evening of that same day Leann would need encouragement far beyond all that any of us could imagine. Now Leann is the one who is most devastated by what has happened to David. Her husband is dead! The father of their lovingly expected baby is gone!

We had agreed with David that his dad and I would come to help as soon as the baby arrived. That is when we expected to see Leann next. I had no idea that I would be bringing my letter to her only the day after its writing.

"David died!" The message I heard on our answering machine keeps haunting me. How is this possible? One minute I am lifted up by my hope in God, the next minute I face the reality of what has happened and I am ready to fall apart. In my heart I keep asking, "Oh, my God! If You are 'building our family,' how can You do it with such a tragedy?"

A question begins to haunt me: "Does God build His family with people who have bleeding hearts?"

Yes, it must be so. Yes, I myself was drawn to the Father when in a message I was shown His beloved Son's bleeding heart, pierced on the cross for me. It was my sin that caused His agony and death! I was convicted to turn from my disobedience and ask the Father to make me into His obedient child. Oh, what it cost God's Son to bring me to the Father! Now as we mourn for David, our bleeding hearts are tasting the anguish of soul that cannot even be compared to what God's Son endured on His cross while He was pleading the Father for our forgiveness. Now we understand more fully His unspeakable love that flows from His pierced heart. His love is now our assurance that even in this tragedy we are the Father's beloved children. Because of Jesus we know that His Father hears our cries for help.

2

God Turns Our Tears Into Hope

Saturday, June 20, 1998

By mid-afternoon we reach Leann's apartment in Ridgeland. Huddled together on her couch, we listen to her as she relates what happened: Yesterday afternoon David, Leann and the children were having a fun-time with neighbors and their children at the crowded swimming pool of their apartment complex. A lifeguard was watching the swimmers' safety.

Everyone knew that David liked to swim under water. But this time someone noticed that he hadn't come up. Immediately the men rushed to him, pulled him from the water and tried to revive him. A kind neighbor lady lovingly whisked Christalyn and Benjamin to her apartment to spare them from the sight. Paramedics arrived, but it was too late. David was dead.

It is unimaginable how David, the expert swimmer of our family, could drown in a small swimming pool. He knew so well how to handle himself under water. While growing up in the Panama Canal Zone, for him swimming was almost a daily experience in the pool or in the ocean. When he trained as a scuba diver he was the youngest and smallest in the group. The trainer praised David's skill in keeping up with the others. We have scrapbooks with many photos of him under water.

To think that tomorrow is Father's Day. What a Father's Day!

My mind drifts to David's last letter, the one in the large white envelope that he handed me at Elise's wedding. He wrote it to help us understand what baptism means to him. Could the manner of how he died be a mere coincidence?

In his discussion on baptism David noted Romans 6:4 in his own writing:

> "Therefore we have been buried with Him through Baptism into death, in order that as Christ was raised from the dead through the glory of the Father, so we too might walk in newness of life." Rom. 6:4

". . . baptism into death . . ." For now these are the only words that stand out for me from this passage. They cause me to tremble in my soul. Baptism by immersion is a picture of the drowning of our old, sinful self. Our son drowned after he wrote these words to me on baptism. But for now "baptism into death," these fateful words are the only ones that my mind is able to grasp. My heart is still blinded by my tears so that I can't see the good news that this passage further declares. A desperate prayer keeps welling up within me, "Dear Lord Jesus, we need You! Please, make it clear to us what Your purpose was in taking our son in this unexpected manner."

The doorbell rings. It is Newell Simrall from Pear Orchard Presbyterian Church, the new church home of David and his family. He has come to pray with us and to comfort us. Oh, how we need a word of sympathy and the showing of concern! We deeply appreciate his kindness! But the Bible passage that he reads to us, Romans 9:20 and 21, does not seem comforting at all. It is rather distressing. In these words God declares that He is the Potter, and we are the clay! God has the right to do with us whatever He wills.

My first impression is that God is warning me not to talk back to Him. I have the feeling that He is commanding me "You have to accept what I am doing with you!"

"Accept this? How can I accept this?" My heart cries out in despair. How can our merciful God hurt me so much? Oh, the loss of our David is devastating to me. How can this be all that God has to say in my search for comfort? Does He not have a word of kindness or compassion to ease my pain? Why is God treating us so?

I open my Bible and look up Romans 9:20 and 21. Looking for hope, I continue reading on in the passage to verses 23 and 24. Oh, yes! God has more to say! God does have words of kindness and compassion for my pain! I have found a hidden treasure! I read it out loud:

> *"And that He might make known the riches of His glory to the objects of His mercy, which He had prepared beforehand for glory, even us, whom He has called . . ."*
> *Romans 9:23, 24a NIV*

" . . . *even us* . . ." Yes, " . . . *even us* . . . ." We are the objects of His mercy. God is speaking to "us." He is speaking to me. Yes, I did hear His call. I do know that I belong to His Son, our Lord Jesus Christ. For me, out of this—a tragic death—God purposes to grant a new understanding of Him and of His compassion. He will make His mercy known to me and to our family. Our Father delights in mercy:

"He heals the brokenhearted and binds up their wounds . .
He takes pleasure in those who fear Him, in those who hope in His mercy." Psalm 147:3

"The Lord is near to those who have a broken heart and delivers them out of all their troubles." Psalm 34:18

"He has not dealt with us according to our sins, and has not punished us according to our iniquities.
For as the heavens are high above the earth, so great is His mercy toward those who fear Him." Psalm 103:10

Tragedy can bring hope along with it. This is one of the mysteries of our walk with Jesus.

Leann's heart responds to the promise I just read. Her last moments with David are triggered to life in her memory. After David had been officially pronounced dead in the hospital, she was left alone with him. There lay her beloved husband whose life in Jesus was wholeheartedly dedicated to the heavenly Father. As she gazed at him, a farewell wish welled up in her heart, according to the fervent desire that he had for his life here on earth, "David, so let your light shine before men,—even now in your death,—as you have let it shine before men in your life!"

David's dedication to the Father made him—in the first place—a wholehearted family man. He was more than a loving husband He was the loving, self-sacrificing father of her children keeping them unceasingly in his heartfelt prayers. With burning heart she assured him that one day, by God's grace, she would meet him together with all three of their children in heaven.

Driving home from the hospital she searched for the right words to say to Christalyn and Benjamin. She noted that God had arranged a most beautiful, brilliant sunset for the closing down of Friday, June 19, 1998, the day that brought the unexpected, drastic turn into her life. It was as if God were saying words of assurance in her heart, "See, life goes on, heaven is eternal and sure. Just as surely as the sun rises and sets, David is with Me. I am smiling on you, Leann!"

As I hear her words God is building hope in me for my family. He is putting us back together. Our risen Lord brings life anew out of death. Somehow, by God's enabling grace, our broken hearts will get to know God in a new way, in His mercy and in His glory. We are to experience the truth of God's written promises in our own lives. The godly life of David, even though cut short, will yet somehow display God's mercy toward our family and leave behind a blessing!

Thank you, Elder Newell, for directing our attention to the written Word of God. What He says to us is a healing balm to our broken hearts. Thank you for the precious prayer you offered up for us. We know that God hears and answers prayer.

Sunday morning, Father's Day, June 21, 1998

At 4 a.m. I find Leann in the kitchen, sobbing in utter hopelessness. For a long while we hug and are unable to speak. We just stand there, our arms around each other and the tears flowing down freely. With aching hearts we ponder the reality of what Leann is facing now.

The first concern is for the baby who is soon to be born. His name will be Solomon Isaac, the name David and Leann had chosen together. But now David is gone. He will not be here to welcome the little one as planned. Christalyn, Benjamin and Baby Solomon are left without a daddy!

This is Father's Day. What a Father's Day!

Slowly we begin to find words to talk. Leann tries to explain the turmoil in her heart,

> "Suddenly I've become a widowed mother! I have to raise my children without a father. I feel like I'm struggling to hold up my apron filled with marbles. I have to keep holding it up to keep them from spilling out. If one falls out then all the others will roll out as I try to pick it up. The more I try, the more will spill out and I will never be able to gather them all up again. I feel totally incapable.

The marbles are all the responsibilities that have now

fallen on me. I'm completely overwhelmed as I think of all the official arrangements that have to be made immediately I don't know how to handle them. David was the one who took care of our daily affairs. I feel wholly unprepared, totally unable to face what is ahead of me."

As we try to talk in the midst of our tears, a heart-cry keeps welling up within us: "Dear Lord Jesus, we are in despair. We need You!"

Leann's thoughts are filled with memories of David: "He was so helpful around the house. He did so much. Even late last night Benjamin discovered, in the freezer, ice cream treats that his daddy had picked up on his way home from work. His last shopping trip was for a surprise to delight the children with a family party after their swim. The ice cream treats are still in the freezer—left behind as a token of his love for us."

Leann calls my attention to the prayer David had written on the title page of his Bible:

Lord make me a servant!

"Everyone knew of David's willingness to be helpful," Leann relates. "Just the other day he was cheerfully lending a hand to neighbors who were moving. Also, it was well known that he was a dad to whom his children were precious. He was always teaching his children to obey God. His heart was so earnestly set on raising our children to the pleasure of God."

Leann notices the tears streaming down my cheeks. She forgets her own anguish as she senses my grief, David's mother's broken heart. She searches among her memories for those that would be a comfort to a bereaved mother. Though I had the privilege of enjoying David in his childhood and youth, Leann is the one who knew him best in his manhood. She shares with me one of David's favorite sayings, one he repeated often, "You have to be all for Jesus, or you are not for Jesus at all."

Then she reminds me, "David first heard this statement from D.J. It brought about a turning point in his life."

It is easy to remember how David and D.J., David Jones, were bonded together from their earliest childhood into a friendship that lasted for life. They were born in the Panama Canal Zone just about the same time, and they grew up together in school and at the Curundu Protestant Church, which our families attended. They shared happy memory after memory of the church's youth group. The delightful youth retreats at Santa Clara Beach have always been pleasant topics of their conversations when we gather together for church reunions here in the United States.

When David's father retired from the Panama Canal Company, our family moved to Bryan-College Station, Texas, where David was to attend Texas A&M University. After his graduation he entered the military and much to his delight he received orders to serve in Panama for three years. His best friend, D.J., was still living in Panama. At church their friendship deepened as they shared their love for the Lord Jesus.

They liked to meet on a hill overlooking the Canal. They sat on a rock and joined their hearts together praying, singing praises, worshipping the Lord and seeking Him in His Word.

Words can't express how deeply we are touched now as we read of those meetings in our "Family Memory Book," a Christmas present to Phil and me from Leann and David in 1987. In it our son himself describes that special meeting when D.J.'s statement changed his attitude toward the Lord Jesus. He wrote:

I know I am a Christian from when I was quite young. I don't remember any specific dates but I do know that I am a child of God. I never was committed to the Christian life the way I am now.

I did not realize how important God is until one day in Panama while I served my Army tour there. D.J. and I were sitting on the side of the hill where the Panama Canal Administration Building is, looking over Albrook Airfield, just below where Dad's office was.

D.J. said, "I now know that either you are all for Jesus or you are not for Jesus at all."

This statement made me realize how important the Christian walk is. It has been very hard seeing the struggles D.J. has been going through.

But I get comfort in the fact that God is working all this to make both D.J. and me more like His Son, Jesus Christ.

Sometimes I wish I could see things the way God does. Someday I will!

David D. Steers
December 23, 1987

David had a special design for his signature. He made the first and the last "S"-s to look like lightning bolts, while the "T" in the middle stood out like a tall cross.

Like David, I don't remember the exact date when he became a child of God. He was about eight years old when, coming home from a puppet show at our church, he told me that he came to Jesus through His promise:

"Every one whom My Father gives Me will come to Me. I will never turn away anyone who comes to Me." John 6:37 TEV

David's lifelong friendship with D.J. blessed Leann. Many times she heard him repeat D.J.'s saying: "You have to be all for Jesus, or you are not for Jesus at all." She says, "Through the years, in their friendship—even after longer separations—they always took up where they left off. David faithfully kept D.J. in his prayers. When D.J. went through hard times David shed tears in his prayers for his friend. This friendship matured David into becoming a man of prayer after God's own heart."

I am so thankful for these quiet, early moments with Leann before the day starts. David's life has special meaning to the two of us, his wife and his mother. We are closest to him through our deep emotions. These precious memories do help us both to find a measure of comfort.

Suddenly, I think of my letter that I had written to Leann on

Friday. It must have a word from the Lord that could help us now. I had spent most of the day writing it before the devastating news startled us into deep distress.

"Leann," I ask, "where is that letter I handed you yesterday? Let's review what God laid on my heart to say to you before the roof caved in on us."

She finds it and we begin to read. It opens with this thought, "All of us mothers have been where you are now!"

What an understatement! Have any of us in our family been where Leann is now? No, not me! I had the comfort of having my loving husband with me when I felt overwhelmed and so inadequate to face the pain of childbirth.

But now here is what Leann is facing: Her husband is dead. Her baby's father and her two other children's father is gone. Gone is the one with whom she shared all the joy and anticipation of their new baby's arrival. Gone, too, is the provider of the family, and it is final. There is no turning back. None of us have been where Leann is now!

We continue to read my letter:

> Shortly before our baby daughter Marion was to be brought into the world by Dr. Archer, I heard these words in my heart:
>
> "Fear not! Your King is coming to you!"
>
> These words put me to rest! These words enabled me to yield my body and my baby into God's loving hands. I was enabled to accept whatever way my King planned to bring our baby into the world.
>
> I had the assurance that my King would come into my life in a new way and into my baby's life by His promised mercies.
>
> Dear Leann, by His Holy Spirit the Lord Jesus will make Himself as real and alive to you as Baby Solomon is real to you inside you right now!
>
> That is if you open your ear and your heart to the very special Word that He is speaking to you right now. He is preparing you for the very special experience with Him

that is before you!

But we have a mighty enemy! The god of this world!

The enemy hates for us to hear God's life-giving Word because it is God's Word that enables us to say, "Father, not my will, but Yours be done!"

That liar will do his utmost to invade our minds and our homes with his lies, with worldly distractions and entertainment, with "busy-ness," with lustful temptations, with self- centeredness. All this is to keep us from hearing our Father's life-giving Word.

It is in God's Word that we see the glory of the Father who raised our Lord Jesus Christ from death to life and who is also able to "raise to new life those who are dead in sin" and "to make them alive to God." 2 Corinthians 4:4-5:1. It is in God's Word that we are shown our very special, individual part that our Savior has prepared for each one of us in His church, which is His body, His family.

Thank God, on His cross God's Beloved Son earned all the favors and all the mercies of His Father for us! Our Father's door is always open for us to come to Him!

"LOOKING UNTO JESUS" WHO WAS ABLE TO ENDURE THE CROSS BECAUSE AHEAD OF TIME HE WAS SHOWN THE JOY THAT WOULD FOLLOW HIS SUFFERINGS.

The Virgin Mary, too, was shown first God's great plan for her life, to enable her to face the sufferings that it would include. This insight is what enabled her to pray: "Let it be to me according to God's Word."

And to us Jesus says the same: "Behold, I send the promise of My Father on you. My Holy Spirit will enable you with power from on high for the task I have for you!" [Luke 24:49 in my words]

His plan is better than all our own plans.

With loving prayers and hugs, Mom Steers

Leann notices one sentence in a special way. She brings it to my attention. "This is prophetic," she says, "Open your heart to the very special Word that He is speaking to you right now. He is preparing you for the very special experience with Him that is before you!"

I had no idea how significant my comment would be. It never entered my mind that Leann would face a heartbreaking horror that same evening.

Leann and I join our hearts and tears together in ardent supplication and then our thoughts return to the reality of the day that lies before us.

Sunday, Father's Day, June 21, 1998

It is time to get the family ready for a busy day.

I plan to fix scrambled eggs for breakfast, but Christalyn offers to do it for us.

"Oh!" I exclaim, "You know how to fix scrambled eggs?"

Christalyn gives a triumphant answer: "Yes, I know how to fix scrambled eggs! My daddy taught me at the Mission where he took me to help feed the homeless people."

I remember well. David took us with the children to the Neighborhood Christian Center a couple of times when we were visiting their family. This was so typical of David! He took every opportunity to be helpful, and he always took his children with him.

The Prince of glory conquered David's heart

Were the whole realm of nature mine,
That were a present far too small;
Love so amazing, so divine,
Demands my soul, my life, my all.

David cut out these lines from the church's song sheet and kept it in his Bible.

Here are the words of the entire song:

"When I survey the wondrous Cross
On which the Prince of glory died,
My richest gain I count but loss
And pour contempt on all my pride.

Forbid it Lord that I should boast
Save in the death of Christ my God.
All the vain things that charm me most
I sacrifice them to His blood.

See from His head, His hands, His feet
Sorrow and love flow mingled down.
Did e'er such love and sorrow meet
Or thorns compose so rich a crown?

Were the whole realm of nature mine,
That were a present far too small;
Love so amazing, so divine,
Demands my soul, my life, my all."

Isaac Watts

EMBER

"A HOME

A WAY FROM HOME FOR SERVICEMEN"
AFFILIATED WITH: OCSC, INC.

Tel: 52:2450

y	Wednesday	Thursday	Friday	Saturday
	2	3	4	5
	9	10	11	12
	16 No Couples Study	17 Singles Bible Study 6:30pm	18 Faith Meal 6pm (fried chicken) Speaker: Jim Anderson	19 W E D D I N G Tom & Dee Dee 7pm at Crossroads
	23 No Couples Study	24 Dinner for all 6pm	25 C H R I S T M A S D A Y HOME OPEN	26 F R E E D A Y HOME OPEN
	30 No Couples Study	31 Dinner 6pm Children's Hour Special Films Communion	1 F R E E D A Y HOME OPEN	2 F R E E D A Y HOME OPEN

Above is a picture of the Christian Servicemen's Home where David was active from 1980 to 1984, while he served in the U. S. Army in Panama.

David kept this part of a calendar in his Bible as a precious memory of the uplifting gatherings he enjoyed at the Home.

While David served in the U.S. Army in Panama, he was active in the Christian Service Men's Home. David took a Cuna Indian friend, Valerio Lopez with him to the Home for Bible Classes. There Valerio received the Lord Jesus as his Savior Valerio gave David the enclosed Cuna language booklet. Valerio remained active at the Christian Service Men's Home after David returned to the U.S.

Friends in Panama tell us that at this time (1999) Valerio serves the Lord by taking the "JESUS Film" for showings on the Cuna Indian Islands.

Nipa Pentaikleket

Watson Goodman urpisatti

Pinsaleket —
Mani ki saleket suli

PAP TUMMAT PA NANAIT KA SOIKLES KUSAT NUETI 43

San Mateo 28:20
teekine An pe mar pa kuti kuo ye, pirka mar perkuet se ye. Pe itto ku mar ye.

Purpar Oyolesatti 21:4
Pap Tummat a mar ka ipya nis otinnoko ye, teekine purkwet perkuo ye, teekine pootl, teekine kwake wile ittoketi, teekine naikpi ittoketi perkuo ye; ar pela itu immar kus malat per nas ye.

1 Pedro 4:12, 13
Kwenat kan sapet ye, ikar pulekan pe witup takket pe mar ki taal sokele mer kelk pe immar kwapiti yop itto mar ye. Ar pur teki sur ye, pur Cristo pa kar ye.

pe aalkpi ittoet pa werku ye, ati pe werku kwichi kue kur mokan ye teekine pe welikwar ittoe kar ye E kanku kaet yooetse tanikkir ye.

San Mateo 6:33
Ar Pap Tummat E soket pa ikar kan se malt inse pe ami ye teekine E ikar nappirrakwat ye, teekine pela we immar kep pe ka merku ma merku ma kuto ye.

San Marcos 9:23
Jesús e ka soikte ye: Sunna na pe kue ittokele perkwappa sun inmar kn ye, tule ulup ki Pap Tummat kelk penku malat kar ye.

This booklet is published as the Lord provides the means in more than 145 languages for free distribution to people EAGER to read. If you can use more copies for prayerful distribution, write to the publisher in English, telling how many you need and in what languages. Published by:

WORLD MISSIONARY PRESS, Inc.
P.O. Box 120
New Paris, Indiana 46553 U.S.A.

VAlerio· Loper
paRA DAViD

David kept
Valerio's booklet
in his Bible

Kuna

3

GOD TURNS OUR TEARS INTO THANKSGIVING

Sunday morning, Father's Day, June 21, 1998

Leann requested that David's memorial service and the funeral be held at Riveroaks Reformed Presbyterian Church in Memphis, where, until their recent move, they were members for nine years.

In Ridgeland our family hurriedly gets on the road to arrive at Riveroaks Church in time for the Sunday worship service. Many members of the church family are already gathered together, and they receive us with open arms. Their tears flow as freely as ours. They share our pain that, for the first time, David is not with us. They deeply feel with us our bewilderment over David's unexpected homegoing. Through His loving people, our God puts His comforting arms around us!

The church family had made arrangements for us to stay at a hotel. The ladies made provision for meals for everyone who would attend the memorial worship and the funeral. Their kindness is overwhelming! Our tears of mourning mingle with heartfelt gratitude, yet I am hardly able to take in all this generosity. The reality of the moment keeps haunting me: "David is dead! He is gone from our midst!"

As we walk toward the sanctuary, in the hallway a vivid picture flashes into my memory. Right here, at this very spot, shortly before David and family moved to Ridgeland, we were together at Riveroaks Church. There in the hallway our young man David had made his way toward us with his joyful smile, carrying his Bible. He was coming to lead us to his Sunday School class. Somehow God made me notice our son in a special way that day. He was so radiant. He was visibly eager to hear God's Word. He was always so happy to be among the people who love the Lord Jesus and His Word.

At the church that they started to attend in Ridgeland, Pear Orchard Presbyterian Church, David was nicknamed "The Man With The Round Bible." Leann had to keep making the cover of his Bible bigger and bigger because he wanted to keep together Pastor Spink's sermon notes and his own handwritten prayers and pictures of missionaries and other remembrances that were so important to him.

Christalyn and Benjamin with their daddy's "Round Bible." He treasured most God's fulfilled promises of the Savior who had come to bless the family

As David grew into manhood the Bible became his most treasured possession. When he was a young boy, while we were living in the Panama Canal Zone and were members of the small Curundu Protestant Church, we knew where David would sit during the church service—the very front row on the right side, closest to the pulpit. Some other boys stayed in the back to carry on playfully, but David was in front listening attentively to the preacher.

When he was three years old, his vacation Bible school class was called to the front to sing "Jesus Loves Me." David sang the words as clearly and loudly as he could, the way the teacher had taught the children to do it. But he was not able to keep up with the older children, so he sang the song at his own pace. When the others were finished, David still had one more line to sing. He sang out his solo with his whole heart: "For the Bible tells me so." The congregation loved it.

When he was eleven years old, David volunteered to give his testimony. He stood on a stool to be seen behind the pulpit as he said, "God showed me that I have been a 'carnal' Christian, but now I want to follow the Lord Jesus with my whole heart."

From 1971 to 1973 the men and women of the Curundu Protestant Church built a new church building in a new location and named it Crossroads Bible Church. David used his free time to join the work with great dedication. I still hear his happy voice when he was operating the back hoe, "Mom and Dad, come and watch me!"

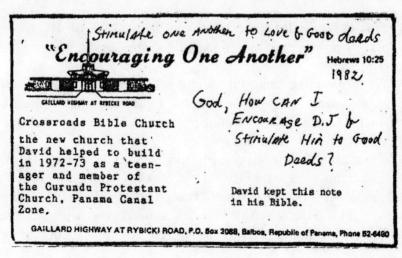

Stimulate one Another to Love & Good deads

"Encouraging One Another" Hebrews 10:25

1982

GAILLARD HIGHWAY AT RYBICKI ROAD

Crossroads Bible Church the new church that David helped to build in 1972-73 as a teenager and member of the Curundu Protestant Church, Panama Canal Zone.

God, How can I Encourage D.J & Stimulate Him to Good Deeds?

David kept this note in his Bible.

GAILLARD HIGHWAY AT RYBICKI ROAD, P.O. Box 3088, Balboa, Republic of Panama, Phone 52-6480

My heart is flooded with precious memories. David left with us his love of going to church and his love for Bible study. It just does not seem possible that David is dead!

Monday, June 22, 1998

Today is visitation, when we "view the departed loved one" at the Memphis Funeral Homes, Memory Hills Gardens. This will be our last look at our son here on earth. For my morning devotion I review John 17, the prayer that our Lord Jesus offered up to His Father at the Last Supper. I have been working on memorizing it.

Suddenly my eyes stop on verse 24 and tears come streaming down. Many years ago our Lord Jesus had already offered up a perfect prayer for the unusual plan He had for David.

Quickly I locate a large sheet of paper and a heavy colored marker. I will take this prayer with me to the funeral home and place it in David's casket.

I write with large letters:

> *"Father, I will that all those whom You have given Me be with Me where I am, that they may see My glory, the glory which You have given Me— in Your great love to Me—before the foundation of the world." John 17:24 NRSV*

This prayer will be a testimony of Jesus' love for His own to everyone who comes to mourn David. This prayer is a treasure from heaven to me.

We arrive at the beautiful Memphis Funeral Home with broken hearts and many tears. Leann's mother and father, Mikie and Mike, her sister, Colleen, and brother-in-law, Todd, are there already. They drove all the way from Indiana.

It is a miracle that our son Philip is able to be with us. He was scheduled this weekend to fly back to Saudi Arabia from his home-leave in California. The news of his brother's sudden death reached him at the last minute so that he was able to change his flights. Our daughters, Yolan and Marion, drove from Atlanta. Yolan's second son, Jason, came with them to play the piano at the memorial service.

As our children arrive, the photos taken at our granddaughter Elise's wedding flash back into my memory. Just about ten days ago all four of our children were together at that happy celebration. David stands out with his contagious smile. How happy we were then!

Once more God has brought our children together, but David is gone! Now only three of our children are here.

Oh no! David is still here. He is in the next room behind the closed doors. We are to "view" him in a few minutes. We are to "view" him in his casket! How I wish I could just run away from here! "Do I really have to go through the agony of having to view him?" I ask myself.

Yes! I must go to see him! In my hand I have Jesus' prayer written in large letters. I have to lay the paper in the casket so that everyone can see what Jesus prayed for David. This prayer is the only way I can go through the torment that is before me.

Pastor and Mrs. Spink arrive. Soon the closed door will open for us. We will go inside and see our precious David laid in the casket, for the first time not able to greet us with his welcoming smile.

Leann—three weeks away from her baby's birth—has to keep greeting the sorrowful arrivals. She is just now receiving hugs from her tearful mom and dad.

Oh, dear! David's five-years-old Benjamin must be stopped from climbing all over the beautiful furniture. Until now it was his daddy who kept watch over his little son. But now? Oh, my heart aches for little Benjamin. The training of this precious, lively little boy will have to continue without a father. What a drastic change has come about in his life by the loss of his daddy! For a long time he will not understand the seriousness of it.

Ten-years-old, Christalyn is already a little lady. To think that she was there when her daddy was pulled out from the pool. Oh, what must be going on in her heart? She loves her daddy so very much.

Finally, the closed door opens to the room where the casket is set up. I feel so weak. I need help! Couldn't we pray together before we go inside?

No, it is time to enter the room. Very slowly, with heart pounding, I enter with the family. There is our son David! The large room is beautiful with the warm glow of dimmed lights, decorated with flowers and fine furniture.

Before I take a close look at our lifeless son, I hurry to find the most obvious place where Jesus' prayer will be seen best. I prop up the paper on the opposite side inside the casket, next to David, where everyone will surely see it.

Now I see his face. He seems so peaceful. It seems like he has a little smile. His hands are lifted up slightly as though Someone had come to raise him up.

There is my David! He looks so real. With his eyes closed he looks as though he is asleep.

He is wearing a colorful shirt of tropical design. He liked such shirts because they reminded him of his childhood in Panama. Leann explains through tears, "David himself chose this fabric when we were at the store. He himself was going to sew it, but with the new job he never found the time. Finally, I surprised him and finished the shirt. We certainly did not intend it for this heartbreaking occasion!"

The elegant room, the beautiful flowers, the dimmed lights, and David's lifelike appearance give such a peaceful impression. But—even with the surroundings of beauty and peace—within my heart a storm is raging. Our full-of-life David is laid to eternal rest. Only his memory will remain present on this earth with us. He is not here to join in with us anymore.

We form a mournful family circle of prayer around our precious David. In loving memory his brother, Philip, has chosen a most fitting passage from the Bible to read to us:

> *I have fought a good fight, I have finished*
> *the race, I have kept the faith.*
> *Finally, there is laid up for me the crown*
> *of righteousness, which the Lord,*
> *the righteous Judge, will give to me on that Day,*
> *and not to me only but also to all*
> *who have loved His appearing."*
> *2 Timothy 4:7,8 NKJ*

Our tearful prayers in choked voices follow. Then in unison we say from memory the closing prayer, our "Family Prayer" of the Psalm, that we consider our "Family Psalm:"

"Search me, O God, and know my heart;
Try me, and know my anxieties;
And see if there is any wicked way in me,
And lead me in the way everlasting."
Psalm 139:23, 24

Then Mrs. Spink takes me aside to the next room and shows me a special passage from the Bible lying on a table:

"Devout men are taken away, and no one understands
that the righteous are taken away to be spared from evil.
Those who walk uprightly enter into peace,
they find rest as they lie in death."
Isaiah 57:1b, 2 NIV

The pastor's wife knows how deeply puzzled I am at the way God summoned our son to Himself by "immersion under water," right after he wrote us that letter about baptism. She explains from God's Word with assurance that our loving heavenly Father must have a merciful purpose in taking David at this time and in this manner.

Then, as in deep thought, I lift my eyes from the Bible, a completely unanticipated miracle unfolds before me.. I watch it with awe. The sight is beginning to lift the crushing pain from my heart. Could it be that what I see has the power to dissipate my inner turmoil into thanksgiving to God?

Mourners keep streaming in to express their heartfelt sympathy. With amazement I see faces that so richly express heartfelt condolence. A sense of wonder comes over me. God is assuring me that our David's life was not wasted. David's earnest aspiration was to bring the joy of Jesus to others. Truly, God has worked and is still working to fulfill this deepest desire of David's heart.

People are filing in: relatives, friends, church family, acquaintances, present and former neighbors, coworkers, a professor and a colleague from Memphis State University where David had studied, his present boss and coworkers from Jackson, cousin Alex from Los Angeles, our granddaughter Elise from Detroit. Some of these people have come from hundreds of miles away. Among the former neighbors are dear Mexican friends who were teaching Spanish to David, Leann and the children.

God has done this! David's dad and I are completely puzzled. How did they all hear so quickly about what happened Friday evening? And today is only Monday! There was such short notice. How did the travelers make arrangements to get here in time? Yes, God has done this.

They have all come to tell us how much they loved David—how much he meant to them, how much they will miss him, how deeply he had touched their lives. We, his family, had no idea that his life had such a lasting impact on so many people around him. They keep giving us a wealth of insights that we never knew about him. This is more of God's healing touch.

With a smile our comforters pour out their pleasant memories of David: "He was a breath of fresh air at work . . . He was a man who truly lived the Bible . . .a wholehearted family man . . . a hard working, excellent employee . . . always ready to cheer people around him . . . a loving, caring neighbor . . . a friend who could be trusted to lend a helping hand." They all remember his smile saying, "He had a unique sense of humor. It was easy to laugh when David was around."

Some former coworkers tell us about a "Western Day" at work when everyone was expected to come dressed as Texas cowboys and cowgirls. David arrived with a surprise, dressed as an Indian. "Cowboys and Indians, you know!" he grinned.

At his new job, our son had to attend a computer seminar. His instructor tells us that David was first to complete the assignments. Then he went around to help those who were slower at understanding them.

The professor from Memphis State University tells us that David was not only his favorite student, but also his assistant. David could always be counted on when he was given an assignment. A colleague from the university came to tell us how he had hoped that he and David could join their efforts to prepare their doctoral dissertations together.

My tears are drying up! Is this possible? I am surprised. I am able to smile! Our son blessed so many people with his buoyant personality.

So many were deeply touched by David's joyful faith in God and cheerful willingness to be helpful. His life spoke of the Lord Jesus living in his heart. His actions spoke of his intimate closeness to God. He left behind no spectacular achievements as our society defines "spectacular," but he was an encourager of loving attitudes among people.

With a chuckle I recall how his dad was always after David to get a hair cut and to dress in a way that would be appropriate for a man with advanced degrees. His friends were puzzled at how he delighted to walk around barefoot. When one of his friends asked him why he didn't put on shoes, he answered with a surprised little smile, "Well, why ask? I don't want to wear them out!"

In our family he was the uncle who enjoyed playing with his little nieces and nephews. He had a way of gathering them around him and leading them in games accompanied with giggles and laughter. He could walk across the room looking like a gorilla, and he could do "The Tigger Dance," making a face just like Tigger's in the Winnie the Pooh video. The little nieces and nephews liked him to take them to the jogging field. One day they were squabbling among themselves because they all wanted to sit in the front seat of the car. Uncle David calmly solved the problem by telling them, "All right, you can all sit in front, and I'll sit in the back." With that he climbed in to sit on the back seat. Dumbfounded the little ones exclaimed, "But then who will do the driving?" Uncle David had an amusing way of getting the children to listen to him.

He used to enjoy introducing his brother Philip's daughter by the name, "my first niece, Elise." She arrives at the funeral home sobbing uncontrollably. Just a few days ago, at her wedding, she had enjoyed his great sense of humor so very much. She is crushed with grief of seeing him in the casket.

After a while, however, as the loving visitors keep telling us of the blessing that David left with them, Elise, too, begins to listen. Soon she brings out her wedding albums and cheers us with the memories of that joyous family celebration to which David added so much with his inspiring personality. Even now David is leaving behind a smile for us.

I return to the casket to spend a quiet prayerful time alone with David. His brightly colored tropical shirt triggers a family memory from the time when David was a teenager. Yolan, his older sister, was helping Marion, his younger sister, to sew a dress. The sisters were amused and surprised when their brother also came to join their sewing circle. To tease them he had purchased some really loudly colored tropical fabric and a pattern for a man's shirt. He was not going to be left out of the family fun. He copied what his sisters were doing and took turns with them at the sewing machine. In the end he had a fine man's shirt, even finishing it before Marion completed her dress. He had never done any sewing before! David had an unusual way of adding cheerfulness and novelty to our family activities.

Now it is time for the funeral parlor to be closed for the night. While loving people were comforting us with memories of David, it seemed that he was there with us just asleep in the other room. But now, again, we have to face the cruel reality. We must leave. The light must go out. David must be left behind alone at the Memphis Funeral Home in his casket, in that room alone in the dark.

The tears begin to flow again. Leann's mom sinks down into an armchair in the corner, sobbing in despair, not able to go on with her grief. It is unbearable! Her daughter's loving husband is gone from her side just now when she needs him most for the birth of their baby. Her children have become fatherless. How can Leann and the children face this tragedy?

Leann rushes to her mother and wraps her comforting arms around her saying, "Mom, this is the path God has foreordained for me to walk and walk it I must! I must hear and obey God's call!" God has brought about a miracle in Leann's heart! He promised His enabling grace, strength beyond natural human ability. Our Lord Jesus promised:

> *"I will not leave you as orphans; I will come to you." John 14:18*

God is enabling Leann to face the test, and by her courage all of us are strengthened. God's beloved Son was enabled by the Holy Spirit to be obedient to the Father even unto death, death by crucifixion. The same Holy Spirit is now working in our hearts to carry us through this present sorrow. He is assuring us that the Father of our Lord Jesus has not turned His love and favor from us. "Fear not," He whispers in my heart, "I am here with you."

Back at the hotel our families gather for evening prayer. Christalyn, who loves to read, asks if she could read to us from her Bible. Her daddy had challenged her to read through the Bible from the beginning. She had been reading faithfully every day. She got as far as the book of Isaiah. Today's passage is from Isaiah 51. Oh, the kindness of God! He arranged our little granddaughter's Bible reading to make her arrive to the exact words that are most timely for us right now:

> *"Awake, awake, put on strength,*
> *O arm of the Lord;*
> *Awake as in the ancient days, in the*
> *generations of old . . .*
> *Are You not the One who dried up the sea,*
> *the waters of the great deep;*
> *Are you not the One that made the depths*
> *of the sea a road for the redeemed to cross over?*
> *Therefore the ransomed of the Lord shall*
> *return, and come to Zion with singing; with*
> *everlasting joy on their heads:*
> *they shall obtain joy and gladness;*
> *and sorrow and mourning shall flee away . . .*
> *I, even I am He who comforts you . . .*
> *I am the Lord your God, who divided the sea,*
> *whose waves roared:*
> *The Lord of hosts is His name . . .*
> *And I have put My words in your mouth;*
> *I have covered you with the shadow of My hand,*
> *That I may plant the heavens, and lay*
> *the foundations of the earth, and say to Zion,*

'You are My people.' "
From Isaiah 51:9-16 NKJ

Christalyn beams with assurance that God's Word will not fail us.

How thankful I am now that David taught his children to enjoy reading the Bible. God will use His Word to hold them up as they realize what the loss of their dad means to their young lives.

My thoughts drift back in time to a scene when Benjamin was just a two-year-old toddler. We were together in their living room with David and Leann seated next to each other on the couch. Benjamin went to the book case and soon came back carrying his picture Bible. He nestled himself between his daddy and mama. Then he opened his Bible and handed it to David saying, "Daddy, read!" He and his daddy had a lively and most enjoyable discussion "reading" the pictures in the Bible.

No wonder that the Lord Jesus wants us to be like little children! Christalyn and Benjamin are an example of how readily we should be drawn to our heavenly Father, who is ever ready to teach us His Word and whose greatest joy is when we gather around Him to hear Him and to obey Him.

Our heavenly Father sent His beloved Son to build Him a family of loving, obedient children. With all their hearts David and Leann wanted to build their own family into such a family, a family of loving children to the heavenly Father.

David and Leann - August 23, 1986

Jesus did not come to tear us down. He came to build us up. Jesus is building us up. I need to keep my heart open.

Jesus keeps building us up together as the Father's family with all those who are going through this sorrow with us. He is in our midst making His Father known to us in a very specially new way.

It is not only our immediate family that is being built up. Our invisible God is building a new bond through our experience with the church family and with the many loving friends whose lives David had touched. Our great God keeps teaching us together His ways, which we never could have known apart from these shared experiences and apart from His written words in the Bible.

I want to work on Acceptance of weakness.
I will choose a Scripture verse (2 Cor 12:9,10) to
Memorize and meditate on.   (Jer 29:11-13)

David Stearns
PG

My behavior
    Doesn't affect my birth
But my birth affects my behavior

Ps. 51:10-12

Create in me a clean heart

Help me start over Again

Restore to me the Joy of Thy Salvation

Oh my God

David kept these
notes in his Bible

4

GOD TURNS OUR TEARS INTO A MIRACLE OF WORSHIP AND PRAISE

Tuesday, June 23, 1998

This is the day of the graveside worship for our family and the burial of our precious son David. Following that sorrowful event we are to attend the "Worship in Memory of David" at the Riveroaks Presbyterian Church, Germantown, TN.

My morning devotion leads me to a new, joyful assurance:

> " . . . One of them, named Caiaphas, who was the High Priest that year, said:
> "You do not know a thing! Don't you realize that it is better for you to have one man die for the people, instead of the whole nation being destroyed?"
> (Actually he did not say this of his own accord; rather,

as he was High Priest that year, he was prophesying that Jesus was about to die for the Jewish people, and not only for them, but also to bring together into one body all the scattered children of God.) " John 11:50-52 TEV

My heart leaps at the words, "but also to bring together into one body [one family] all the scattered children of God, the Father . . . " Our Lord Jesus died not only to take away our sin but also to gather us together into a family of loving, obedient children to His Father. Today's Scripture brings new hope to my heart. It confirms Jesus' wonderful words to me on the morning before David was taken. On that fateful morning I wrote in my diary: "We are Jesus' family. Stand on the final outcome! Jesus is Victor!" These words are His enabling grace whereby I can face this day of mourning and grief.

Very thoughtfully Pastor Spink had arranged the private graveside worship for David's family to take place in the morning. Then the memorial service at the church would take place at noon so that many of the congregation could attend and afterwards remain for lunch hosted by the ladies of the church. Their hospitality would provide for us time for unhurried visits with family and friends.

In the morning our family meets at the beautiful Memory Hills Garden. The Lord has prepared a blessed, sparkling, sunny day for us. On trembling feet we move toward the graveside tent, where Pastor and Mrs. Spink with Pastor and Mrs. Williams are waiting for us.

But who are the other people standing with them welcoming us with open arms? Surprise! They are longtime friends, Dr. Leslie Archer with his wife, Naomi, and D.J., David's childhood buddy and lifelong, closest friend and prayer-partner. We all were members of the Curundu Protestant Church during our happy days in the Panama Canal Zone. My heart is filled with gratitude to these very special loving comforters who came from far to stand with us at this painful time.

Dr. Leslie Archer was the doctor who delivered our baby Marion. He and Naomi drove from Chattanooga to be with us. D.J. traveled all night by bus from Colorado, where he attended the Curundu-Crossroads Bible Church reunion this weekend. How great for D.J. to arrive in time all the way from Colorado to his friend's funeral in Memphis, TN.

How kind God is! He planned David's homegoing while so many who had loved him at our Panama church were together at a reunion! Immediately, when the news reached them, they joined together in prayer for us. This is another confirmation from God that He had called David home at His perfect time, according to His predetermined, eternal plan.

We take our seats facing the open casket. The lifeless form of our precious son offers a startling contrast with the field of beautiful wild flowers surrounding him with their dazzling colors in the sunshine. In the midst of death God reminds me of His power to give life. I fix my eyes on the paper that I had placed next to David yesterday written with the prayer of our Lord Jesus:

> *"Father, I will that all those whom You have given Me be with Me where I am, that they may see My glory, the glory which You have given Me—in Your great love to Me—before the foundation of the world." John 17:24 NRSV*

This prayer will keep wiping away the tears of my heart until that joyful day when I see our son again. The memory of seeing our David in the casket will indelibly stamp Jesus' prayer into my heart.

How is it possible that just last Friday morning David woke up full of life, looking forward to the weekend? But now the worst is to come. The casket containing his handsome earthly body will be lowered down into the ground, never to be seen again. How could I bare this pain without Jesus?

Leann whispers to Christalyn and Benjamin. Hesitatingly they rise and walk forward. They carry the Father's Day cards they had designed and colored last week while their daddy was still with them. With Leann's encouragement they approach the casket in reverent silence. Then they place the cards next to their daddy's quiet body and hurry back to their seats into their mother's arms.

What a way to celebrate Father's Day!

Then Mike, Leann's dad walks over to the casket, holding a

small wooden cross in his hand. He is a skilled carpenter by hobby. He turns to us and says, "Last week I made several small wooden crosses as gifts for a special event at my church. I found that I had enough wood for an extra cross. While I was working on it I was wondering why God had placed an urgency in my heart for one more since I did not need another one. Now I understand!"

Tearfully Mike places the cross into David's hands. Again Mike turns toward us to say with deep sorrow, "David has touched our family and our lives with his example. He is my son in Christ, he is my brother in Christ, a true Christian who carried his cross.

This morning, as I read my Bible, I found comfort in these words:

> *'And David comforted . . . .his wife . . . and called the baby's name Solomon . . . and the Lord loved him.' 2 Samuel 12:24*

I pray that David's wife, our precious Leann, will be comforted with the consolation that God alone can give her."

As Mike returns to his seat, David's father stands up. He reads from his Bible 2 Timothy 4:6-8, the passage that the Lord had laid on his son Philip's heart the previous night. His voice is choked with tears as he draws special attention to the last verse:

> *"Finally, there is laid up for me the crown of righteousness, which the Lord, the righteous Judge will give me on that Day, and not to me only, but to all those who have loved His appearing."*

With effort, this grieving, heartbroken dad adds, "How grateful I am knowing that our son David is among those who have loved Jesus. He was looking forward with joy to the appearing of our Lord Jesus in glory. Now David is—beyond any doubt—among those who are singing praises to the Lord in His very presence."

Then Pastor Spink steps forward to remind us of our Lord Jesus' admonition:

"Feed on Me till I come."

The pastor reminds us that we feed on Jesus when we treasure up God's Word in our heart. We feed on Jesus who became a human being just like us and lived with us here on earth and died for us here on earth and returned to His glory. Jesus understands all our sorrows. The promises of God that the pastor reads are like manna from heaven to my soul so famished for strength. The promises remind us that we who love the Lord Jesus are not to grieve like those who have no hope. We expect Him, our risen Lord and Savior, to come for us in the clouds in glory. He will bring all our loved ones with Him. So shall we ever be with the Lord. Our hope is in God:

"Precious in the sight of the Lord is the death of His saints." Psalm 116:15

"There is no condemnation to them that are in Christ Jesus . . . " Romans 8:1

As the pastor concludes his exhortation D.J. stands to speak. It is D.J. who had made the life-changing statement to our David, "You have to be all for Jesus, or you are not for Jesus at all." He is so grateful to David for having kept him faithfully in his prayers all these years, even with tears at times, while they were apart.

D.J. brings greetings from those attending the Curundu-Crossroads Church reunion: "The last song we sang, "My Anchor Holds," is still ringing in my ears. That title fits my best friend, David, so well. We all can say with him, "My Anchor holds!" We can say it, in spite of our tears, because Jesus is our never-failing Friend. This is what the Bible says of Him:

'. . . having loved His own who were in the world, He loved them unto the end . . .' John 13:1"

Dr. Archer is next to stand up. He tells us of his very recent conversation with David and Leann. At the end of May he and Naomi attended the graduation of our grandson, Philip IV, from The McCallie School in Chattanooga, TN. They cherish the memory of their unhurried chat with David. Dr. Archer adds, "David was a young man without guile, with nothing to hide. He was all out for the Lord Jesus. God must have taken him because he was so ready to be taken home to the Father's house. If Jesus had not risen from the dead, we would have no hope for our grief. But Jesus is risen from the dead! We look forward with expectation to seeing Him and we will see our loved ones with Him."

Then Pastor Williams comes forward and reads Scripture passages of our Almighty God who rules over all and who always does what is right:

> *"Shall not the Judge of all the earth do right?"*
> *Genesis 18:25c*

> *"The steps of a good man are ordered by the Lord."*
> *Psalm 37:23a*

> *"In Your book . . . were written . . . .the days You have ordained for me . . ." Psalm 139:16c*

Pastor Williams is glad to share how much he enjoyed David as one of his students in his Sunday school class. "David was my most enthusiastic student. He always sat on the front row and was first to find the Bible passages that were being studied. He anticipated the questions that would be asked and was ready with the answer practically before they were asked. David was zealous for the Word of God. He loved the Lord Jesus and His Word."

The pastor chuckles as he remembers how much David loved to sing. When the congregation was invited to request their favorite hymns David liked to ask for the song "He Holds The Keys," a hymn based on Revelation 1:18. Then he joined in the singing with his whole heart—noticeably off key—yet inspiring others with his enthusiasm.

"I am convinced," Pastor Williams adds, "that David was willing to say with Jesus,

> *"Shall I not drink the cup which My Father has given Me?" John 18:11b*

The two pastors invite us to join our hearts together with them in prayer. Then we are given a little more time of silent meditation before the lid of the casket is to be closed. I take a last anguished look at our son's lifeless body. How can the tears of my heart ever dry up at this memory?. It seems like I hear my heavenly Father saying to me:

> You are weeping over the lifeless body of your son.
> Have you wept for the crucified body of My beloved Son?

I confess that I have wept for my sin and my shame that took Jesus to the cross. But I have not wept for His pain. He gave His best for my worst! The pain I feel now for my son is nothing compared to the pain JESUS suffered for me. I shudder and grieve at what my son may have gone through there in his death "immersed under water." But I never understood as I do now how JESUS must have suffered when He died for my sin and the sin of the whole world. What He suffered in His crucifixion is too awesome for my limited understanding to comprehend.

I shudder as I consider what is foretold in prophecy of Jesus' return when the whole world will weep:

> *" . . . they will look on Me whom they have pierced;*
> *and they will mourn for Him, as one mourns for an only*
> *son, and they will weep bitterly over Him, like the bitter*
> *weeping over a first-born. . . ." Zechariah 12:10, 11a*

Oh, how I have wished that I would never have to see the sight of a precious child of mine lifeless in a casket. Oh, how the pain of David's last moments under water haunt me! My son was taken away without my consent. But God's Son gave Himself away of His own free will.

In my loss now I am beginning to know Jesus "in the fellowship of His sufferings." My pain is nothing compared to the agonizing love with which He sacrificed Himself for me.

The officials of the Memory Hills Garden walk up to the casket, and then, very slowly, as gently as possible, with reverent silence, close the lid. The thud sounds like thunder in my heart. The funeral is over. David is dead! Life will never be the same.

We are being ushered away from the horror of having to see the casket being lowered into the ground. My legs can hardly carry me, I am so shaken. D.J—with deep compassion—draws close to Phil and me to remind us with gentle words, "David is not in that casket. What we saw is only his temporary home in which he walked for 40 years. David is now with Jesus, alive forever!"

The words of a precious hymn strike up an old melody in my heart:

> Were you there, when they crucified my Lord?
> Were you there, when they nailed Him to the tree?
> Oh, Oh, Oh, sometimes it causes me to
> tremble, tremble!. . .
> Were you there when they nailed Him to the tree?

This is the song that brought me to my Savior and Lord, Jesus Christ, many years ago. My heart is filled with a fresh glow of wonder at what He did on the cross for me. Oh, how much more deeply I understand now what He did for me to take away my sin! God's beloved Son was crucified! He, too, was dead and buried.

Then we are taken to the Riveroaks Church for the memorial service. As we enter, we are handed the church bulletin:

"Riveroaks Reformed Presbyterian Church, Germantown, TN

Tuesday, June 23, 1998

A SERVICE OF WORSHIP IN MEMORY OF DAVID DWIGHT STEERS

January 9, 1958 - June 19, 1998"

"David Dwight Steers!"

I stare at the name in disbelief, "A Memorial Service" for our David? Is this really happening to our son? Is this solemn occasion really for our David? How can this be?"

Our family, Phil and I with Philip, Yolan, and Marion, and Leann's family, her parents, Mike and Mikie, with Leann, Christalyn, Benjamin, Colleen and Todd, are seated on the front rows. Jason stays near the piano, ready to play when he is called.

David is missing. David always sat with us in this church. "David Dwight Steers" from now on is a memory. Oh! How can I take it in?

The church is filled to capacity, the entire choir is assembled in the choir loft. Again, I marvel at how David meant so much to so many people. After the beautiful piano prelude, Pastor Williams gives the call to worship:

"We are the flock under our Father's care.
Rejoice in God's presence! Rejoice in God whose

presence David is enjoying now!"

> *"O come, . . .Come, let us worship and bow down: Let*
> *us kneel before the Lord, our Maker.*
> *   For He is our God;*
> *And we are the people of His pasture,*
> *   and the sheep of His hand.*
> *Today, if you would hear His voice,*
> *Do not harden not your hearts . . ." Psalm 95:6-8a*

We sing the solemn hymn of worship, "Holy, Holy, Holy." Then Pastor Spink offers a prayer of thanksgiving to God, knowing David's love for God's Word. He knows beyond a doubt that David is gone to glory and that he is now filled with the eternal pleasures of seeing the Living Word, our Lord Jesus, in glory.

While the choir exalts God with a beautiful hymn of adoration, I glance back toward the entrance into the sanctuary. "What if David would walk in?" The thought stirs within me. In my heart I could see him walking down the aisle—as usual—with his "round Bible" and with his joyful smile. "If only . . . ! I sigh. "No, David can't walk in again!"

"But Jesus did! He did!" The thought comes as a ray of light.

After His body was wrapped in grave-clothes and after He was placed in the tomb. . . . after He was dead! Jesus did walk in. His shattered disciples were gathered together in despair. Three days have passed. All hope was gone. The Man who had promised them eternal life was dead! Then there He was! Jesus walked in . . . ALIVE! . . . What joy! Now I see the miracle!

Even though we can't see Him, Jesus is here with us. He is making Himself known in a new way in my heart. He is here in the hearts of this loving church-family selflessly gathered together to bring consolation and encouragement to David's bereaved family. The words of John 11:50-52 from my morning Bible reading come back to me with deeper meaning:

Jesus died not only for the Jewish people, but also to bring together in one body [one family] all the scattered children of God, our loving Father in heaven.

Then Pastor Spink walks to the pulpit and begins his message from John chapter 17, Jesus' prayer at the Last Supper. My heart skips a beat. This is the chapter I have been memorizing lately. It is from this chapter that I copied out my treasure, verse 24, Jesus' prayer for David, to place it next to him in the casket:

"Father, I will that all those whom You have given
Me be with Me where I am, that they may see My glory,
the glory which You have given Me—in Your great
love to Me—before the foundation of the world."

"Many years ago," the pastor begins, "at the Last Supper, the Lord Jesus prayed for David. All the good that was in David's life was the Father's answer to His Sons prayer. All glory belongs to the Lord Jesus who loved David and gave Himself for David. Jesus started His prayer with this request:

'Father, glorify Your Son that Your Son also may glorify
You . . .
Holy Father, I pray . . .for those whom You have given
Me, for they are Yours.
All mine are Yours, and all Yours Mine and I am glorified
in them.'

"Here is how the Father answered His Son's request for David: When David came to Jesus as a young boy, the Lord Jesus received him, and the Father gave him to Jesus. David gave testimony of his faith that Jesus died for him. Glory has come to Jesus by David's assurance that Jesus has received him and that He has washed away his sin with His precious shed blood. Jesus continues His prayer:

'Father, now I am no longer in the world, but these
are in the world, and I come to You.
Holy Father, keep through Your name those
whom You have given Me . . .
Now I come to You, and these words I speak in the
world, that they may have My joy fulfilled in themselves.'

"Our eternal joy is being with Jesus. David displayed great joy in getting to know Jesus through His Word. David's smile and his zeal showed that he had found his joy in Jesus. David testified of his conviction that joy can be found in Jesus alone. David found great joy in being a servant of the Lord by being helpful to people. Jesus' prayer continues:

"Father, I have given them the words which
You have given Me . . .
I have manifested Your name to the men whom You
have given Me out of the world . . .
They are not of the world, just as I am not of
the world . . .'

"David was a young man detached from the world. He was not conformed to the ways of the unbelievers. He was not consumed with worldly passions.

"David was a man of one purpose. He was not distracted from his one purpose in life. That one purpose was to prepare himself to live in God's eternal home, in the heavenly Jerusalem, whose architect and builder is God. David was ready! Jesus had prayed for him:

'Father, sanctify them by Your truth,
Your word is truth.'

"God's truth in the Bible thrilled David because from its good news he received the assurance that he was created for Jesus and was kept for Jesus. David rejoiced in knowing that Jesus had bought him for Himself at the great price of His own precious shed blood. This is why he treasured the Bible. He did not just carry it around, but found delight in living according to the great truths that are taught in it.

"He was faithful in attending the weekly Men's Bible Study and Prayer Group. He was known for his heart-searching questions whereby he challenged the men to deep thought and great anticipation in searching the Scriptures. God heard Jesus' prayer:

'Father, as You sent Me into the world,
I also sent them into the world.'

"The Word of God touched David to have a deep compassion for people around him. His heart was touched with their need to get to know Jesus. He was willing to go out of his way to reach them for Jesus.

" David brought his neighbors' children to church. His confident attitude was infectious. He participated with great zeal and dedication in the work of the missions committee at Riveroaks Church. He prayed fervent and personal prayers for the missionaries, mentioning them by name. His desire was to qualify for service on the mission field.

"Jesus' next prayer can be David's own prayer for his family:

'Father, now I am no longer in the world but
these are in the world, and I come to You.
Holy Father, keep through Your name those whom
You have given Me, that they may be one as We are one."

"David's deepest dedication was to his family, the loved ones whom God had entrusted to him to be his responsibility. David's most cherished promises were the ones God had given him as father of his family.

'Holy Father, keep through Your name
those whom You have given Me.'

"David took this prayer with him, hidden in his heart. He is now in the presence of the heavenly Father presenting this prayer in person to Him.

"Next, the Lord Jesus presents the most urgent concern of His heart to the Father:

'. . . that they all may be one, as You,
Father, are in Me and I in You; that they also may be one

in Us, that the world may believe that You sent Me.
And the glory which You gave me I have given them,
that they may be one just as We are one . . . . '

"David loved the church. David loved to be in church. He simply, gladly took part in the activities. He never tried to outdo others. He was cooperating, not competing. He was grateful and content, instead of being critical. He simply enjoyed being present. At Riveroaks Church David certainly had an important part in strengthening the unity of the church.

"The next words in Jesus' prayer fill our hearts with deep gratitude for they are just right for David's present moment:

'Father, I will that all those whom You have given Me
be with Me where I am, that they may see My glory, the
glory which You have given Me – in Your great love to Me
- before the foundation of the world.'

"This is the glory of God's children—to see Jesus in His glory! The Father in heaven has answered His Son's prayer for David!

"This is what God did for David, He made him into a convinced Christian young man who lived a simple, obedient life. God did not ordain him to make a great name for himself in this present world. God ordained him for our Lord and Savior Jesus Christ to make a great name for Himself through David's zealous dedication to Him. It is Jesus' mighty work that made him zealous for God. It is Jesus who receives the honor in David's heart and conduct.

"The mighty work of our Lord and Savior Jesus Christ in his life brought pleasure to the heavenly Father and a challenge to the people around him. Even now - as we review his life—he is cheering us on in our own walk with the Lord Jesus.

"Now, in closing, let us be thankful and praise God with joy that the prayer of our Lord Jesus at the Last Supper is His prayer for us all! So then, let us express our thanksgiving to our Father by rededicating ourselves to live for His pleasure."

Truly, Leann's parting words to her beloved husband were heard in heaven:

"David, so let your light so shine before men,—even now in your death,—as you have let it shine before men in your life."

Instead of a service of grieving tears as I had expected, this was a service of worship and praise to our heavenly Father for what He has done in our son's life in answer to the prayer of His beloved Son, Jesus.

Appropriately the next hymn is "To God Be The Glory," an unusual choice for a memorial service.

CRisto
Nombre Glorioso
Precioso Salvador
Bello Senior

Emanuel
Dios con Nosotros
PALAbRA Viva VIVA
Libreventor
& LIBERTADOR

Most Important – Jesus
Remember what He did
VS 10
By the Blood
Confidence to enter the
Holy place
Bread / Flesh / Veil
new & living wAy
we have A great
high Priest
ONce For All

Phil 2:3
consider one another
As more Important than
Yourself

whatever you have done to
the least of these you
have done unto me

Consider others As Jesus

Do not merely look out
for Your own interests
but the Interests of others

**David
kept
these
slips
of notes
in his
Bible**

GOD USES THE ORDINARY
TO ACCOMPLISH THE EXTRAORDINARY
Please read Nehemiah 2: 17-18

"Then I said to them, 'You see the trouble we are in:
Jerusalem lies in ruins, and its gates have been burned
with fire. Come, let us rebuild the wall of Jerusalem, and
we will no longer be in disgrace.'

Nehemiah 2: 17

David kept this message in his Bible. It is so fitting for him.

The people of God under the leadership of Nehemiah had a huge project on their hands—to rebuild the wall that surrounded Jerusalem. Archeology teaches us that this project was an immense undertaking. The people of God faithfully stood shoulder-to-shoulder against all odds to complete the wall in only fifty-two days.

There were no stone cutters, masons, or engineers listed, only regular folks like us. This is consistent with the way the Lord builds His Kingdom and His Church. He doesn't use just experts. He uses Moms, Grandfolks, kids', business people, teachers, doctors—all of His people working together. By His grace He uses the ordinary to do the extraordinary.

T. Durant Fleming
Minister to Young Adults

How does God carry out His eternal plan?
With awe-inspiring wonders by the power of His hand?
Sometimes.
How does God execute His perfect decrees?
With angels and archangels for all to see?
Sometimes.
But more often than not, and it's a mystery to me;
He uses regular people like you and like me.
Imagine that.

We know that God loves ordinary people because
He made so many of them

69

5

THE SOLEMN WARNING
THAT DAVID LEFT BEHIND

Tuesday, June 23, 1998

At the "Service Of Worship In Memory Of David Dwight Steers" is approaching the time for the closing prayer I cling to the refrains of the great hymn of Jesus' triumph "To God Be The Glory." But then, suddenly, I am wrenched from the heavenly heights to face, once again, the reality that God has taken David from us.

There is a stirring at the seats closest to us. Leann and her two little ones move to the front. Christalyn and Benjamin are closely clinging to their mother. Standing before the gathering is the widowed mother, great with child, her arms around her two father-less little ones—left behind. How can I hold back the tears?

A hush comes over the congregation. Leann, with steady voice, upheld by our God's enabling grace, shares a request:

> Baby Solomon Isaac will never know his
> father in person. It is only from what we tell him
> that he will know his daddy. I ask those of
> you who have memories of my husband to write
> them down for me.
> I will appreciate your kindness so very deeply.
> I will cherish all the memories that David left behind.
> My children will only really know their daddy
> from what you and I share with them.

How very much our family will miss David! "Yes," I agree, "memories of David must be written down." They must be preserved in writing while they are still fresh, not hurriedly though, but with much prayer and heart-searching. I must do my part to help my precious grandchildren to remember their daddy."

As the grandmother of Christalyn, Benjamin and Baby Solomon my fervent prayer is that they will get to know Almighty God as their loving heavenly Father. They will need firm confidence that our Almighty Father has a loving purpose in taking their daddy from them at such an early age.

I must support Leann in every way as she assures the children that our heavenly Father always works what is for our eternal good. They need such faith in God that will enable them to face life without an earthly father.

But how can I leave behind the praises of our Almighty Father for my precious grandchildren when He has torn my heart to pieces? I am the mother of their daddy. It is my son for whom we are in mourning with our family. Leann's request to write down memories of their daddy sends me to my knees.

It takes much searching of God's Word, first of all for myself, to understand more clearly His dealings with me. Then, together as family we need insight from God about what His purpose is for us in this tragedy. God's ways are higher than our human ways. He alone can give us understanding to recognize His love toward us in this overwhelming trial.

When I first heard the cruel news of our son's tragic death, I wondered how I could carry out God's command posted over my kitchen sink. It sounded like a contradiction:

> *"In everything give thanks, for this is the will of God (your Father) concerning you."* 1 Thessalonians 5:18

Now however, I must admit, that since the shattering news, step by step, God has led us into circumstances that fit together like a puzzle especially prepared for us. First of all, He surrounded us with loving people who are standing with us with fervent prayers, efficient help and consolation. Through them He is assuring us of His changeless love for us.

Next – to my surprise—I find that David himself is comforting me. An unusual comment of his flashed into my mind. He was five years old. I was teaching his Kindergarten Sunday School Class. I asked the children, "Why did God send the flood?" I expected the children to reply, "Because the people were so bad." But David chirped up before the others and gave this surprising answer:

God sent the flood to make Noah's ark float!

How timely these words are to me now in my flood of tears! He seems to be telling me, "Remember, Mom, my ark floats. My ark is our risen Lord Jesus Christ in glory. I am now safe and secure in His loving arms. And remember that your ark floats, too. Your ark, also, is our Lord Jesus, who floated Noah and his family safely through the worst flood that ever hit the earth."

Noah listened to God's warning of the coming judgment. He carried out God's specific instructions for building the ark. When the flood came, his ark was ready and he saved himself and his family.

Thank God, the testimony that our son David left behind for us gives us the evidence that he was like Noah, obedient to God's Word. Sadly, our own day also reminds us of the days of Noah before the flood. While Noah was busy building the ark to save his family, his neighbors had no time for God. They fell for the devil's lie: "You have time."

"And they did not know until the flood came and swept them all away, so will be the coming of the Son of man." Matthew 24:39 RSV

Even we, too, never expected our son to be taken from us so suddenly. We were sure that David had lots of time ahead of him. I recall how, at Elise's wedding, Phil and I talked together saying that "at our age" we must enjoy every moment with our four children. "At our age," we mused, "we can't know whether this will be our last time together as a family." We had always expected that one of us two, the old ones, would be taken first. Who would have thought that the Lord picked our full-of-life David to be the first in our family to be called home? And the Lord called him just a few days after our happy days together.

Yes, we all thought that David had lots of time. How powerfully his sudden death brings Jesus' warning to our attention:

"Watch therefore, for you do not know at what hour your Lord is coming.
Therefore you also be ready . . ." Matthew 24:42, 44 NJK

"Watch therefore and pray always . . ."
Luke 21:36 NKJ

How thankful we are to God that He had faithfully worked in David's heart to prepare him for His sudden homecall! David's conduct did show evidence that he took to heart God's warning that He is coming to pour out His wrath on the disobedient. David knew that Jesus' coming in glory will only bless those who have obeyed His Word but will be a disaster to those who have not listened to God's warning of "His wrath to come." This is what the Bible calls "The terror of the Lord." 2 Corinthians 5:11

Even as a young boy, David had a tender, teachable spirit like Noah's, whose "ark did float." An incident from David's elementary school days shows how he became a wise and obedient son who brought pleasure to his parents. His dad had been warning him that if he brought home a bad grade in cooperation from school, he would have to get a spanking. That dreaded day for the promised punishment arrived. Oh, how we all wished that it could have been averted! David's dad—as much as he hated to do it—kept his word. He gave his son a spanking not soon to be forgotten. Then father and son prayed together. That evening—at family devotions—David said a prayer that would remain written in my heart:

> Dear Jesus, thank You that I have a father
> who teaches me to do right.

While David's little sister, Marion, heard the blows on her brother's "board of education" and the accompanying cries coming from him, she hid under the kitchen table. "I'll never disobey daddy!" she resolved, and she never did need a spanking. Little children often are wiser than grown-ups. God used Marion's big brother David for a solemn warning, whereby she made sure that she would never have to face her daddy's displeasure by disobeying him. From then on loving correction was sufficient to discipline her.

David, too, was smart enough to heed his dad's unforgettable warning. He never needed such a spanking again, even though, being a normal boy, he did need firm training all along.

We as parents have found the secret for good results in child training. We can testify that the faithful teaching of God's Word, along with much earnest prayer, is more powerful and effective than any spanking. David learned early that his dad could not spare him when he disobeyed. All our children were taught what our heavenly Father had to do—sacrifice His beloved Son to die on the cross—in order to save us from "the wrath to come:"

> *Our Father "did not spare His own Son, but*
> *gave Him up for us all . . ." Romans 8:32*

Along with this solemn warning our children were also taught that:

*". . . he did not spare the ancient world . . . when he
brought a flood upon the world of the ungodly." 2 Peter 2:5
" . . .through which the world that then existed was
flooded with water and perished" 2 Peter 3:6*

At this thought, once more, I am perplexed and my heart trembles. God, who did not spare His beloved Son and did not spare the ancient world, even so did not spare our beloved son, David. Could it be that God dealt with our son in the same way as He did with the disobedient people in Noah's day? Oh, no! David was obedient just like Noah. In a mysterious way the circumstances of his death have a message to us. David's remark as a little boy about Noah's ark floating in the Flood and his last letter about the meaning of baptism and our Lord's calling him home by "immersion under water," all seem to fit together in a mysterious way. And there is even more.

To my happy surprise I discovered that even the apostle Peter teaches that "God sent the flood to make Noah's ark float:"

*" . . . the few people in the ark—eight in all—were
saved by the water.*

*This water was a figure pointing to baptism, which
now saves you, not by washing off bodily dirt, but by the
promise made to God from a good conscience.*

*Baptism saves you through the resurrection of Jesus
Christ, who is gone to heaven and is at the right side of
God, ruling over all angels and heavenly authorities and
powers." 1 Peter 3:20b- 22 TEV*

Noah and family were saved by the water! The flood made their ark float! The flood that destroyed some people, turned out to be a blessing to those, who obeyed God. In my mind I see the death of Jesus as though He had gone down into the flood to drown with those who perished:

*"For Christ died for sin once and for all, a good man
on behalf of sinners, in order to lead you to God."
1 Peter 3:18 TEV*

Jesus, the only Innocent Man, went down into death just like those who deserved to be punished, in order to bring them to God. Our David went down into the same kind of death immersed under water. I marvel how God took him in this manner at the same time when he found deep assurance in God's Word that he had been united to Jesus in baptism. There is so much mystery here. I must cling to Jesus, our risen Lord, because He is David's and our "Ark that floats.

There is another most unusual circumstance that fits into God's perplexing plan for David's unexpected homecall. The pastor of his new church, Pastor Kalberkamp of Pear Orchard Church, over several Sundays, brought a series of messages alerting his congregation to be ready for the unexpected return of our Lord Jesus. As part of this series the pastor had already prepared a message for the Sunday that would turn out to be the one after David's funeral. In that Sunday's bulletin he had given it the title, "The Door Will Be Shut: Then What Will You Do?" It is based on Matthew 25:1-13, the parable of the wise and foolish virgins.

The alarming homecall of David turned out to be a heartrending, solemn illustration from God for the warning this faithful man of God was proclaiming. The pastor received permission from Leann to speak of David by name. God used David to give the congregation His own warning by so suddenly and unexpectedly snatching him out from among them.

How thankful Leann and the children were when the pastor in his sobering message was able to describe their family's daddy with these words:

> David was a man of joy. He lived his life with zeal and with enthusiasm. He always brought a smile with him to cheer up the people around him.
> The joy was deep in his soul, because he was confident that he belonged to the Lord Jesus, and that Jesus was living in his heart.

Then Pastor Kalberkamp, with tearful eyes, kept asking his congregation: "How about you? Are you ready for the Lord to come for you?"

"The door will be shut: Then what will you do?" Even the title fits the example of how Noah and his family escaped the flood, while the others perished. God declared:

> *"For behold I, even I, do bring a flood of waters upon*
> *the earth, to destroy all flesh . . . .*
> *But I will establish my covenant with you and you*
> *shall come into into the ark, you, your sons, your wife and*
> *your sons' wives with you . . .*
> *And Noah did all that the Lord commanded him.*
> *And the Lord shut him in.*
> *The flood continued forty days . . .*
> *and the ark foated on the face of the waters."*
> *Genesis 6:17, 18; 7:16, 18 RSV*

"The Lord shut him in, . . . and the ark floated."

"The Door Will Be Shut . . . " was the pastor's message. In Noah's day only one family was safe inside the door when it was shut. God's judgment became a blessing to the obedient, but for the rest of the people outside the door:

> *". . . the flood came and swept them all away."*
> *Matthew 24:39 TEV*

I keep searching for more complete understanding of the solemn warning that our God is leaving behind for us all by the way He took our son to Himself. We are thankful that David is able to say, "My Ark floats!" And his family is able to say that David was obedient like Noah. He, too, was a father who was diligently building his family-life on God's Word:

> *Whoever comes to Me, and hears My sayings and*
> *does them, I will show you whom he is like:*
> *He is like a man building a house, who dug deep and*
> *laid the foundation <u>on the rock.</u> And when the flood arose,*

*the stream beat vehemently against that house, and could
not shake it, for it was founded <u>on the rock.</u>" Luke 6:47,
48 (emphasis added)*
" . . . and that Rock was Christ." 1 Corinthians 10:4c

Leann, Christalyn, Benjamin, Solomon can see from David's
well-used Bible and from the last letter that he wrote, and from the
memories that he leaves behind, that he built his family <u>on the Rock,
our Lord Jesus Christ, God's Eternal Word to us.</u> Our almighty
Father is worthy of our trust for the precious family that David left
behind, even now, in this most unusual plan that He had for him.

Our Almighty Father is worthy of our trust even now, because

*" Father of the fatherless' and "Defender of
widows' is God in His holy habitation."
Psalm 68:5 NKJ* (my spelling and punctuation)

The age old hymn now rings in my heart with new meaning:

> Rock of Ages, cleft for me,
> [Ark of Ages, built for me,]
> Let me hide myself in thee:
> Let the water and the blood,
> From Thy wounded side which flowed,
> Be of sin the double cure,
> Save from wrath and make me pure.
>
> Could my tears forever flow,
> Could my zeal no languor know,
> These for sin could not atone:
> Thou must save, and Thou alone:
> In my hand no price I bring,
> Simply to Thy cross I cling.
>
> Nothing in my hand I bring,
> Simply to Thy cross I cling;

Naked, come to Thee for dress,
Helpless, look to Thee for grace;
Foul, I to the fountain fly,
Wash me, Savior, or I die!

While I draw this fleeting breath,
When my eyes shall close in death,
When I rise to worlds unknown,
And behold Thee on Thy throne,
Rock of Ages, cleft for me,
[Ark of Ages, built for me,]
Let me hide myself in Thee."

Augustus M. Toplady, Thomas Hastings

When The Master Plucks A Rose

Read: 2 Corinthians 5:1-9
*"We are...willing rather to be absent from
the body and to be present with the Lord...."*

The death of a loved one or friend is never easy to accept. But as Christians we can rejoice through our tears if that loved one knew the Lord Jesus as his Saviour. We can be assured that God has specifically called another of His precious children to dwell with Him. The labours of that one are completed, and the heavenly Father has lovingly transported him to heaven as a trophy of His redeeming grace. What comfort that is for us who sorrow and are left behind!

The story is told of a nobleman who had a lovely floral garden. The gardener who tended it took great pains to make the estate a veritable paradise.

One morning he went into the garden to inspect his favorite flowers. To his dismay he discovered that one of his choice beauties had been cut from its stem. Soon he saw that the most magnificent flowers from each bed were missing.

Filled with anxiety and anger, he hurried to his fellow employees and demanded, "Who stole my treasures?" One of his helpers replied, "The nobleman came into his garden this morning, picked those flowers himself, and took them into his house. I guess he wanted to enjoy their beauty all day."

The gardener then realized that he had no reason to be concerned because it was perfectly right for his master to pick some of his own prize blossoms.

Has the Lord God plucked a cherished rosebud or lovely bloom from your garden and taken him or her to the mansions above? Rejoice that your loved one is now radiantly happy. Be comforted by realizing that to be absent from the body is to be present with the Lord.   - H.G.B. –

God wants some lovely flowers
For His garden up above!
That's why He takes His children
To the mansions of His love.

– Bosch –

Thot: Death to the Christian means heaven, happiness and God!

6

GOD USES OUR TEARS
TO BUILD HIS FAMILY

Tuesday afternoon, June 23, 1998

The Memorial Service Of Worship moves on to the closing
prayer. With bowed heads and trustful hearts the congregation
joins Pastor Spink in prayer for God's presence to fill us all with the
comfort that He alone can give. Everyone present remembers David
with a sense of loss. The pastor trusts God to fill up the void that is
now in Leann's and the children's lives. Together we look to the
heavenly Father to make Himself known to us in a new way.

Jason, our grandson, takes his seat at the piano. For the postlude
he chose to continue playing on the piano the hymn "To God Be
The Glory." It is the expression of his own gratitude and love for his
Uncle David, who left behind an exemplary testimony.

After the service, the heartfelt sympathy of our friends brings a
healing touch to us as they put their loving arms around us. The
ladies of the church are ready to serve lunch. They are inviting

everyone to stay and enjoy the fellowship around the delicious meal they have prepared. Their generous hospitality is a token of God's love to us.

As we fellowship, friends share how God comforted them when they had experienced grief in their own lives, when they, too, had to walk through the valley of tears. It was in the midst of their trials that they could experience God's enabling grace to continue a meaningful life.

Pastor Williams' voice is choked up as he tells us that his father died when he was eight years old. His mother, alone, had to raise him with her two other children. David Triplett's tears run down as he remembers that he was ten years old when his dad died and his mother was left with three sons. These brave widowed mothers bless us with their example of courage. Through their godly training these faithful men are now serving the Lord in His church.

David's life at his work impacted many people. The executive director of his company came from Nashville to the memorial service to express his sympathy to us. Also, Pastor Kalberkamp and Pastor Presley from David and Leann's new church in Jackson drove up to Memphis for the memorial worship. They have come not only to express their condolences to us, but also to get to know Marion, David's sister. Her brother, as a new member, became known for his persistent requests for prayer for her as she has been going through a most difficult time of testing with her family.

Pastor Kalberkamp is touched beyond expression by the way God has snatched David out of his congregation. This is when he tells us that several Sundays ago he started a series of messages on Jesus' unexpected coming in glory. For this coming Sunday the title of his sermon is already in the bulletin challenging his people to receive God's free gift of a cleansed life before He shuts His door of mercy. The pastor deeply feels for Leann and the children who are to be present on Sunday for the preaching service. She graciously gives the pastor permission to include God's sudden dealing with David into his exhortation, even though it will extend her sorrow. In a mysterious way God had chosen her husband, the father of her children to prove the truth of the pastor's message. What a solemn warning David left behind for us!

"I can tell you how I remember David best," recalls Pastor Kalberkamp. "Our church had scheduled a workday, but the city woke up to a torrential downpour. I was sure that no one would be able to come and help with the projects. To my surprise David walked in with Christalyn and Benjamin in spite of the storm. David greeted me with his usual smile, exclaiming, 'Where is everybody?' Nothing could stop David when there was an opportunity to help. And he always included his children in his helpful activities. God had heard his prayer, 'Lord, make me a servant.'"

Then I share with Pastor Kalberkamp, "We learned only now—after David's homecall—something we didn't know about him. A lady missionary friend, who now serves the Lord in Mexico, finished high school while attending our church in Panama. To the joy of the congregation she was accepted by the Wycliffe Bible Translators for training. David was a teenager then and without our knowledge he contributed to this young lady's support from his own newspaper route earnings." David's concern for family went beyond his own family toward all of God's family.

As we continue to enjoy our fellowship at the luncheon, Pastor Presley joins us. We are delighted to meet him because David has told us that he has a great sense of humor. It turns out that the pastor holds the mutual opinion of David and Leann, referring to them as "the couple who enjoy sharing laughter with others."

Regretfully, the clock is ticking away too fast on our gathering. Once more it is time to say good-bye to these dear friends who have blessed us beyond measure. We depart looking forward to the written memories that will come to Leann from those who knew David. How will we ever be able to thank Riveroaks Church for their overwhelming, unforgettable hospitality toward us? They are a living example of how God uses the caring people of His family to put His loving arms around His afflicted ones. God is working according to the words I read yesterday morning in John 11:50-52,

> *. . .that our Lord Jesus died not only for our sin, but also to gather us together to enjoy our unity as children of the same heavenly Father.*

In this fellowship in memory of David we have experienced that truly the Lord Jesus is our peace and unity. While I lived in sin, I was alienated from God and was not able to enjoy such deep, heart-to-heart fellowship with others. But when I received Jesus into my heart, He washed me from my sin in His precious blood and the Father received me into His blood-bought heavenly family. This is the reason I now truly enjoy being with Him and His children to hear His Word and to worship Him.

How can I thank this loving church for all the compassion and care that they have showered on us in our time of grief? I express my gratitude by a word of prayer for all the heavenly Father's loved ones in His family, the church. I join my heart with the apostle Paul who wrote this prayer:

> *"When I think of the wisdom and scope of His plan I fall down on my knees to the Father of all the great family of God—some of them already in heaven and some down here on earth—that out of*
>
> *His glorious, unlimited resources He will give you the mighty inner strengthening of His Holy Spirit.*
>
> *And I pray that Christ will be more and more at home in your hearts, living within you as you trust Him.*
>
> *May your roots go down deep into the soil of God's marvelous love; and may you be able to feel and understand together with all of God's people, how long, how wide, how deep, how high His love really is: and to experience this love for yourselves, though it is so great that you will never see the end of it or fully know and understand it.*
>
> *And so at last you will be filled up with God Himself.*
>
> *Now glory be to God who by His mighty power at work within us is able to do far more than we would ever dare to ask or even dream of — infinitely beyond our highest prayers, desires, thoughts or hopes.*
>
> *May He be given glory forever and ever through endless ages because of His master plan of salvation for the church through Jesus Christ. Ephesians 3:14- 21 LB*

Wednesday, June 24, 1998

How can I face this day, another day of pain? Our family is to gather together around our David's fresh grave to say farewell to one another. I dread having to go back to the cemetery.

When we left from our last family gathering at our granddaughter's wedding, we said our farewell with happy smiles and happy hearts. Now we are choked up with tears. It still does not seem possible that our family is completely changed.

The Lord prepares my heart for the day by calling me to believe Him like Abraham did:

> *"Abraham . . . believed God, who gives life to the dead . . ." Romans 4:17*

God was pleased with Abraham's faith and "he was accepted as righteous by God." Romans 4:22 TEV. And God is pleased with me when I believe that He raised up Jesus, our Lord, to new life after He was dead to proclaim the truth that God is our life even after death. I face the day with this treasure in my heart from Romans 4:17-25:

> Our God raises to new life those who are dead in body.
> Our God raises to new life those who are dead in sin.
> Our God is pleased with me when I believe Him.

Leann and the children are still busy at the hotel with her family. There are so many family matters that have to be settled. Leann's Mom will stay until the baby comes. The others have to drive back to Indiana.

We are so thankful to God that our son, Philip, was able to change his flight schedule—by God's grace—to come to the funeral. God sent him in answer to Leann's concern about the official matters she would not know how to handle. Philip has the expertise to lead Leann's family through the labyrinth of official actions needed to be undertaken for the widow and her children.

For our parting prayer at the cemetery, the beautiful Memory Hills Garden, we gather with our immediate family, Philip, Elise,

Yolan, Marion, Jason and our nephew Alex.

As we walk toward David's grave, it is difficult to pick it out from among the others. Our first sight of it is a shock. It is just a pile of dirt with a bouquet of flowers. This grave is all that is left behind of our son's physical presence in our midst. I shudder as I realize what will happen to his handsome young body now buried in the ground. "You are dust, and into dust you will return." These words strike me like a sword with their reality.

Without Jesus how hopeless I would be! Without Him how meaningless life would be! Our risen Lord Jesus alone has words of hope for us:

> " , , , *because I live, you will live also." John 14:19b*

> If I believe Jesus, I will see the glory of God. John 11:40

In this valley of tears Jesus is binding our hearts more closely together as a family. Because a precious member was taken from us, we now have a deeper understanding of how each member is a special treasure. God's Word keeps strengthening my heart:

> Our God raises to new life those who are dead in body.
> Our God raises to new life those who are dead in sin.

> I believe that in Jesus death brings resurrection life.

God heard my prayer for enabling grace. My eyes turn to the beautiful wild flowers that God made me notice yesterday all around us at David's open casket. Their dazzling colors are a contrast to the tiny, unimpressive seeds that they were before they fell into the ground. They were buried into the earth and they died. But God sent His sunshine and His rain on them and caused them to germinate to new life. Then the tiny seeds blossomed out and produced these magnificent flowers that have more seeds for planting new ones. It takes time to reproduce new life, but it will surely come to pass.

Jesus compared His Word to a seed. Just as a seed sown into the ground germinates to new life, even so His word sown into a receptive heart will sprout out to eternal life in the body of that believer. Our son David had received God's Word, the Good Seed, into his heart with great joy. The apostle Peter explains what this means to David now:

> " *For you have been born again not of seed which is perishable but imperishable, that is, through the living and abiding word of God. For,*
> '*All FLESH IS LIKE GRASS,*
> *AND ALL ITS GLORY LIKE THE FLOWER*
> *OF GRASS.*
> *THE GRASS WITHERS,*
> *AND THE FLOWER FALLS OFF,*
> *BUT THE WORD OF THE LORD*
> *ABIDES FOREVER.'*
> *And this is the word which was preached to you.*"
> *1 Peter 1:23-25*

Our precious David's body now buried in the ground, enables me to understand the miraculous, life-giving power of God's Word sown into the human heart. In David's body that imperishable seed of God's Word is now buried in the ground. But because of God's Word hidden in his heart, this dead body will hear the wonderful, commanding voice of Jesus that had power to bring Lazarus forth from his tomb. David shall hear the call of our Lord Jesus and come forth in his body by resurrection unto eternal life.

In His kindness, God chose for me this saddest place on earth, the grave of my son, to show me the power of His Son's death and resurrection. He assures me of Jesus' triumph over death and the devil, who has the power of death. My hope is in Jesus! I cling to His Word instead of giving in to my own grief. I must keep my eyes on Jesus and believe Him for the final outcome. Oh, I know that the pain of going on without David will always be with us. But God is giving me eyes to see Him in a new way and ears to hear Him in a new way.

Nothing compares to the promises we have in Jesus.

Our family gathers to hold hands as we join in a time of tearful prayers. Who would have thought—only a few days ago—that this is where we would have our next family gathering?

There is a new assurance in my heart that our Father has bound the hearts of our family more tightly together. I know that our prayers for each other will be more deeply heartfelt. I know that each one of us will appreciate in a new way every precious moment that we can spend together as family.

Now we make our way slowly toward our cars, which will take us in different directions. We take some quick family photos, then we hug. Having to take our leave from one another is always the least desirable part of our time together.

Presently Philip is to catch his return flight to Saudi Arabia. Elise is to fly back to Michigan and Alex to California. Marion, Yolan and Jason start their drive back to Atlanta. Phil and I begin our return trip to San Antonio, where we are to await Leann's call announcing the birth of Baby Solomon. The melody of one of my favorite songs rings in my heart:

He giveth more grace when the burdens grow greater,
He sendeth more strength when the labors increase,
To added afflictions He addeth His mercy
To multiplied trials His multiplied peace.

When we have exhausted our store of endurance,
When our strength has failed ere the day is half done,
When we reach the end of our hoarded resources,
Our Father's full giving has only begun.

His love has no limit,
His grace has no measure,
His power has no boundary known unto men,
For out of His infinite riches in Jesus,
He giveth and giveth and giveth again.

Author Unknown

Let Thy goodness, like a fetter,
Bind my wandering heart to Thee;
Prone to wander, Lord, I feel it,
Prone to leave the God I love;
Here's my heart, O take and seal it
Seal it for Thy Courts above
                    Amen.

Is 53:3
— Man of Sorrows! what a name for the Son of God, who came
Ruined Sinners to reclaim: Hallelujah! what a Savior!
— Bearing Shame & scoffing rude, In my place condemd He stood,
Sealed my pardon w/ his blood: Hallelujah! what a Savior!
— Guilty, Vile, and helpless we; Spotless Lamb of God was He;
Full atonement! can it be? Hallelujah! what a Savior!
— Lifted up was He to die, "It is finished!" was His cry
Now in heav'n exalted high: Hallelujah! what a Savior!
— When He comes, our glorious king, All His ransomed home to bring
Then anew this song we'll sing: Hallelujah! what a Savior!

Te Vengo A Decir
//Te vengo a decir// O mi Salvador
/Que yo te amo+i//Con el Corazón
// Te vengo a decir// Toda la verdad

David kept
these songs
in his Bible

91

7

DAVID'S LAST LETTER—
LEFT BEHIND

June 25, 1998

Phil and I have quiet days in San Antonio while we are waiting for Leann's call announcing the baby's arrival. I concentrate on gathering memories of David.

He was full of life at Elise's wedding, on June 6, 1998, when he handed me the large white envelope with an important, personal message to me. As I reach for it now, a thought, like a dagger, pierces my heart. These are David's last words to me! Do I have the strength to read his letter again now, after the agony of his funeral? To me, a mother, my deepest love is for my children. Will his words add further to my questions and pain after what has happened to him? How can I have confidence that the rest of my children and all my grandchildren are safe in this terribly dangerous world?

But I must not fail him! In this letter David is addressing what has become his last request to me. What he wrote is deeply meaningful to him and to Leann because they are explaining how they have reached the decision to have their expected baby baptized. Since, as I have said, in our family we did not have the custom of baptizing our babies, David shared with me in great detail the study he and Leann made in God's Word concerning baptism. When I first read his letter, I expected to have plenty of time to discuss his and Leann's deep convictions more fully. But with David this will never be.

With a sigh to God for His enabling grace, I set out – in spite of my heavy heart—to reflect deeply on what he has written. Oh, how thankful I am that I did not give in to my hesitation! Again – to my surprise—it is David who brings me comfort concerning the future of all our children. How glad I am that I was willing to study for myself the many Bible passages from which God spoke to Leann and David concerning their baby. Through his deep study of God's Word David leads me to the joyful assurance that, yes, even after what has happened to him, and, yes, even in this terribly dangerous world, I can be sure that my children are secure in the loving arms of our heavenly Father.

As I reach into the envelope for the handwritten pages, my fingers first reach a booklet entitled, "Infant Baptism." David had xeroxed it and enclosed it with his letter. I am about to set it aside for later, but then, on the back page I notice David's handwriting with large letters:

We must obey God!
And so be blessed!

As for me and my house we will
be Baptised and serve the LORD!

[He liked to write "Baptize" and "Baptism" with a capital "B," showing the importance of this sacrament to him.]
Tears flood my eyes. I can't read on. I have to wipe my eyes

over and over before I am able to continue.

"We must obey God!" What a statement of firm submission to divine authority! This was our son's attitude of heart when God took him. Wholehearted obedience to God is all that mattered to him, in order to rest in His divine approval. David wanted to please God, no matter what the cost. "And so be blessed!" What resolute assurance that God would not fail to bless his obedience! He was willing to accept whatever way God would handle his life because He could be trusted to bring about the right final outcome. Is there anything better that I, David's mother, could desire for him?

I marvel as I meditate on the next statement. He had adapted it from Joshua 24:15c. "As for me and my house...." David understood his responsibility toward his family. As father he would have to set the example in order to include his whole family into that obedience to assure God's favor and approval to be resting on all of them together. He determined to aim for God's best for his loved ones.

But why did he pause when he only got halfway through the quotation: "As for me and my house we will (ser) . . .?" He was only halfway through the word "serve" when he crossed it out and wrote instead: "We will be baptized ." Apparently he wanted to express more clearly what was on his heart.

David understood baptism as the first step in obeying God. I am amazed at the words he added as he quoted Joshua 24:15c: "We will be baptized . . . " Could this be prophetic? God took him first from among us and He took him by "immersion under water," the manner in which our family understood that the sacrament of "believers' baptism" is to be administered! Oh, how I long for a clearer insight into God's dealing with us!

Then David continues, "As for me and my house we will (ser . . .) be baptized and serve the Lord." To him baptism is to be a pledge of obedience to God for "family obedience" in order to enjoy "family blessing." With deep emotion I puzzle about what may have been going on in his heart as he wrote these words.

I set aside the booklet on "Infant Baptism" for later and spread out David's letter before me. Now I must face the reading of David's last words to me. This is his answer to a study that I had sent him earlier. I tremble within me as I begin reading:

Thank you, Mom,
Thank you for the study on "Under-
standing Baptism." It was very helpful in
helping me to understand and study what I
really believe God wants me to understand
about Baptism. I have studied the paper
you sent. I also read a booklet by John
Sartelle that I am enclosing. These studies
have confirmed what I believe.
I hope and pray that you will under-
stand Leann and me in our point of view
and be able to rejoice with us at the
Baptism of Solomon Isaac and remember
from Acts 2:39: "For the promise is to you
and to your children.." (Underlined by David)

His underlined words and his emphatic introductory remarks touch me deeply:." to understand and study what I really believe **God** wants me to understand about Baptism . . ." David read his Bible prayerfully to keep as a treasure the words that God Himself would speak to his heart. This is how God enabled him to bring me the joyful news from Peter's sermon on Pentecost Sunday: "For the promise is to you and <u>to your children</u>." This promise that David would embrace at Solomon Isaac's baptism, taken together with verse 38 reads like this:

> *"Then Peter said to them, repent and let every one of you be baptized in the name of Jesus Christ for the remission of sins, and you shall receive the gift of the Holy Spirit.*
> *For the promise is to you and to your children and to all who are afar off, as many as the Lord our God will call." Acts 2:38, 39*

The gift of the Holy Spirit! What a mighty promise! Oh, how important our children are to God! I am filled with gratitude as I reflect on the magnitude of God's promise. It is to me, an ordinary mother and to my children. The Holy Spirit is given to me as a gift. God expects me to receive His love-gift. Even before I knew anything about the Holy Spirit He brought me to Jesus. He also brought David as a young boy to Jesus and Jesus did not turn us away. Now David, as loving father, is bringing his baby son to Jesus. We can be sure that Jesus will not turn him away. I trust our Father's work through His Holy Spirit to bring to Jesus all our children and grandchildren, too. The letter continues:

> *To me the most important is to accept the doctrines from the New Testament and to be able to understand their roots in the Old Testament.*
> *I accept all of God's Word, not just part.*
> *Some teachers mistakenly say that "all of those Old Testament ceremonies are gone, and that the Old Testament is gone." No, these ceremonies, the Passover, circumcision, sacrifices, the various feasts, etc. are not gone, but are fulfilled. Jesus came to fulfill.*
> *No! The covenant with Abraham is EVERLASTING! See Genesis 17:7. God did this for Abraham..* (emphasis by David)

David had learned to understand what God says to him by interpreting Scripture with Scripture. He took to heart "to accept the doctrines from the New Testament and to be able to understand their roots in the Old Testament." David referred me to Genesis 17:7 because in the message that Peter proclaimed at Pentecost of the coming of the Holy Spirit, David recognized this Old Testament promise made to Abraham:

> *"And I will establish My covenant between Me and you and your descendants after you throughout their generations for an everlasting covenant, to be God to you and to your descendants after you." Genesis 17:7*

To Abraham the promise is:

> *"And I will establish My covenant . . . to be God to you and to your descendants after you." Genesis 17:7*

To us, in Christ Jesus, Abraham's Great Descendant, the fulfilled promise is:

> *" . . . you shall receive the gift of the Holy Spirit. For the promise is to you and to your children . . . " Acts 2:38b, 39a*

In his Bible over Genesis 17:7 David wrote with red:

> *Key Promise: God's covenant with Abraham is an EVERLASTING covenant.*
> *Everything Abraham had was from God and he acknowledged it.*

David's letter continues:

> *The Old Testament ordinances are not gone, as some say, they are fulfilled: See Matthew 5:17, 18.*
> *Jesus came to fulfill, not to abolish, the Law or the Prophets. To properly understand the two ordinances that the Lord left for us, we must understand their roots in the Old Testament.*
> *Passover—the Lord's Supper, Circumcision—Baptism.*
> *As relates to Baptism and Circumcision see Colossians 2:8-15* [double underline by David)

I stop to reflect on David's statement: " . . . to properly understand the two ordinances that the Lord left for us, we must understand their roots in the Old Testament: "Circumcision—Baptism.."

Is circumcision really the root of our baptism? I did not know this. I must refresh my memory and look up God's words to Abraham:

> *"No longer shall your name be called Abram, but your name shall be Abraham; For I will make you the father of a multitude of nations . . .*
>
> *And I will establish My covenant between Me and you and your descendants after you throughout their generations, for an everlasting covenant, to be God to you and to your descendants after you . . .*
>
> *. . . I will be their God . . .*
>
> *This is My covenant, which you shall keep, between Me and you and your descendants after you: Every male among you shall be circumcised.*
>
> *And you shall be circumcised in the flesh of your foreskins; and it shall be a sign of the covenant between Me and you . . .*
>
> *As for Sarai your wife, you shall not call her name Sarai, but Sarah shall be her name.*
>
> *And I will bless her, and indeed I will give you a son by her . . .*
>
> *Sarah your wife shall bear you a son, and you shall call his name Isaac; and I will establish My covenant with him for an everlasting covenant for his descendants after him." Genesis 17:5, 7, 15-19*

" . . . you shall call his name Isaac . . ." The name "Isaac" catches my eye and I am struck to the heart. This is the middle name, that David chose for the baby boy whose birth he and Leann were awaiting with great anticipation. Clearly, he chose this name to express his faith in God's promise to Abraham concerning his descendants. He must have been challenged by the faith of Abraham and Sarah, who were at the age when it was humanly impossible to have a baby. But Abraham believed that God would bring life out of his own body that was as good as dead, and that Sarah's barrenness could not hinder God from giving them the baby

boy, whom God Himself named "Isaac." David must have understood the deep meaning of this name and wanted to be reminded of
it in his Baby Solomon Isaac.

As for me, in my deep mourning over the loss of our son David,
the name Isaac makes me shudder. Later on, God required Abraham
to offer up this miraculously born son, Isaac, on the altar as a "burnt
offering" or "holocaust." God, the Father, allowed this earthly
father to understand the pain of His "Father-heart" when He offered
up His own beloved Son in our place on the altar of obedience as
our "burnt offering." Abraham was circumcised not merely in his
body, but God "circumcised" or "cut into" his heart, also. Then God
rewarded Abraham's obedience by providing him with a ram to be
placed on the altar instead of Isaac.

> *"And God said: . . . now I know that you fear God,*
> *since you have not withheld your son, your only son*
> *from Me . . .*
> *By Myself I have sworn, declares the Lord, because*
> *you have done this thing, and have not withheld your son,*
> *your only son, indeed I will greatly bless you, and will*
> *greatly multiply your seed as the stars of the heavens, and*
> *as the sand which is on the seashore; and your seed shall*
> *possess the gate of their enemies.*
> *And in your seed all the nations of the earth shall be*
> *blessed because you have obeyed My voice."*
> *Genesis 22:12, 13, 16-18*

Jesus spoke of Abraham's obedience with these words:

> *"Abraham, your father rejoiced to see My day and he*
> *saw it and was glad." John 8:56 NKJ*

God gave our David such rejoicing faith. It must have been God's
approval of Abraham's obedience in his dealing with his son, Isaac,
that prompted our son to make the heart-penetrating statement:

We must obey God!
And so be blessed!

The words that God spoke to Abraham cut deeply into my bleeding heart, also:

> "... *since you have not withheld your son ... from Me ... indeed I will greatly bless you ... because you have obeyed My voice ...*"

Would I have withheld my son from God had He given me the choice? Yes! Before I was led into this study, I would have rather chosen to keep my son for myself. Among my tears I hear God calling me to trust Him the way Abraham did and the way our son David did.

Returning to David's letter my heart is better prepared to search further. I must find out now from the New Testament how our baptism relates to the Old Testament circumcision. I read,

...as relates to Baptism and Circumcision, see Colossians 2:8-15. (Double underline by David)

I open David's Bible to Colossians. There are markings in it with red and blue ink. He must have studied it thoroughly. Next to Colossians 1:18 David wrote: "Key verse, the Supremacy of Christ:"

> "*Christ is the Head of the body, the church; and He is the beginning, the firstborn from the dead; so that He Himself might come to have first place in everything.*"

David wanted God to be pleased with him in order to secure His blessing on all his family. No wonder that Colossians 2:8-15 was so meaningful to him in his search to understand baptism. He directs my attention to verse 8 with an opening statement:

First of all notice verse 8: Baptism must be 'according to Christ,' not according to human traditions:

"See to it that no one takes you captive through philosophy and empty deception, according to the tradition of men, according to the elementary principles of the world, rather than according to Christ."

David was not satisfied with human wisdom. With a prayerful heart he wanted to know what God Himself was teaching him. Reverently I read on to find out how circumcision relates to baptism:

> *"For the full content of divine nature lives in Christ, in his humanity, and you have been given full life in union with him. He is supreme over every spiritual ruler and authority.*
>
> *In union with him you were circumcised, not with the circumcision that is made by men, but with Christ's own circumcision, which consists of being freed from the power of this sinful body.*
>
> *For when you were baptized, you were buried with Christ, and in baptism you were also raised with Christ through your faith in the active power of God, who raised him from death.*
>
> *You were at one time spiritually dead because of your sins, and because you were Gentiles outside the Law. But God has now brought you to life with Christ! God forgave us all our sins." Colossians 2:9-13 TEV*

Oh, the thrill of being reminded of this good news, "In union with Christ, you were circumcised, not with the circumcision that is made by men, but with Christ's own circumcision, which consists of being freed from the power of this sinful body." This is what He did for me in His crucifixion!

Many years ago a faithful pastor presented to my spiritual eyes God's Son crucified, suffering the agony and torture that I had caused Him by my sin. This awesome sight "circumcised," or "cut away" all the desire from my heart to continue in disobedience. My sinful self was buried with Christ, buried just like our David was buried. Then through my faith in our risen Lord Jesus Christ I was brought to new life with Christ! I was forgiven all my sin.

When Abraham believed God, he was given the sign of circumcision as a seal, that God would fulfill His promise to him. When I believed in Jesus Christ, crucified and risen for me, God gave me the sacrament of baptism as a public witness that He took my old sinful self with Him into His death and that, as my risen Lord, He has made me into a new person to the glory of God, the Father. In the gift of His Holy Spirit Jesus gave me a clean and happy heart as His unchanging promise.

But Jesus has done even more for us than merely forgive us our sins. The next verses that David asked me to look up in Colossians bring more glad insight. It is rooted in the promise God made to Abraham when he was willing to offer up his beloved Isaac on the altar:

> "... *your seed shall possess the gate of his enemies."*
> *Genesis 22:17c KJ*

I know that Abraham's Seed in the first place is his great Descendant, Jesus, whom God promised him. And Jesus' enemy and our enemy is the devil. The next verses in Colossians, that David asked me to look up, declare how Jesus accomplished His promised triumph over our sin and over the devil:

> "*He cancelled the unfavorable record of our debts, with its binding rules, and did away with it completely by nailing it to the cross.*
> *And on that cross Christ freed himself from the power of the spiritual rulers and authorities: he made a public spectacle of them by leading them as captives in his victory procession." Colossians 2:14, 15 TEV*

This is the mighty God that our David chose to obey in order to assure His blessing on his family. He is the God I, too, want to trust. Oh, the happy news! Jesus nailed to His cross all that God requires of me to accomplish and He obtained God's forgiveness for all that I have ever failed to accomplish. Our Father delights in releasing me from all guilt for the sake of His beloved Son's sacrifice for me. No longer has the devil power to accuse me for my failures. God knows that by my own efforts I am unable to overcome my self-centered desires or to produce anything good. But now, the glorious, risen Lord Jesus Himself lives in my heart by His Holy Spirit to overcome all the temptations and accusations that the devil can raise against me. From now on God only requires my gratitude for all that Jesus has done and promises to do within me. His Word assures me:

" . . . *you are complete in Him, who is the head of all principality and power." Colossians 2:10*

The next part of David's letter is a further meditation on his statement: "As for me and my house we will be baptized..." God's Word taught David that baptism is to be the testimony of a heart-unity with God:

The study you sent me considers Romans 6:4 as 'the most explicit picture of the spiritual reality that Baptism visualizes:'

"'Therefore we have been buried with Him through Baptism into death, in order that as Christ was raised from the dead through the glory of the Father, so we too might walk in newness of life."

However we must read on. The best way to understand the spiritual reality of Baptism is to use God's Word. We must again examine God's Word more closely. We must not stop with verse 4, we must continue and look at verse 5:

"For if we have become united with Christ in the likeness of His death,

certainly we shall be also in the likeness of His resurrection."
"We have become united with Christ."
Here then is the truth. Baptism is considered 'union' in the Bible."

"We have become united with Christ." David believed the miracle of Romans 6:5, God Himself provides the obedient heart for His children, which is the basic requirement for baptism. God has heard his prayer to be united with His purposes according to His Word. David's letter continues:

Baptism does not merely consist of someone being submerged, dunked, immersed into water.
There is much more. Baptism means "being counted into union."
In the Bible God performs baptism also without the use of water. Jesus expresses this truth in His words:
"Can you drink the cup I must drink? Can you be baptized in the way I must be Baptized? Mark 10:38"
Here , Jesus calls His death on the cross His baptism.. This was not water baptism.
Also, in 1 Corinthians 10:2 "all Israel was baptized into Moses," meaning that they were counted into union with Moses.
In Galatians 3:27 we read: "'or all of you who were baptized into Christ have clothed yourselves with Christ,". . ."you have put on Christ,"...you were immersed into Christ.
The emphasis here is on what the Holy Spirit did, not on the water that was used.

David understood baptism to be the believer's testimony of his assurance that "God has counted him into union" with our Lord

Jesus Christ because He is:

> *"The Lamb of God, who takes away the sin of the world! . . .This is He who baptizes with the Holy Spirit . . . " John 1:29, 36*

> *"For by one Spirit we were all baptized into one body, whether Jews or Greeks, whether slaves or free, and we were all made to drink of one Spirit." 1 Corinthians 12:13*

David believed God's Word that God had counted him into union with His beloved Son, and he did not want to keep this joyful assurance to himself. His loved ones must be included into this joy, the joy in Jesus, the joy of belonging to Him and to His family, the joy that Abraham knew. David believed that it is "family obedience" that assures the resulting "family blessing." In his letter, next he points out from the New Testament that entire households were baptized to express "family obedience" in order to be received as a family into God's family:

> *Lydia, in Acts 16:15, had her whole household baptized.*
> *The jailer in Acts 16:33 "immediately was baptized, he and all his household."*
> *The household of Stephanas was also baptized in 1 Corinthians 1:16.*
> *During those days probably there were many more Baptisms of entire households than just the ones mentioned in the Bible.*
> *When those households were baptized, was it possible that unbelievers and children were also baptized?*
> *By just one person becoming a believer brought a blessing on everyone in the household including the unbelievers and their children. WOW!*
> *All are blessed - (1 Corinthians 7:14) this*

goes back to God's promise to Abraham in Genesis 12:3."

Notice the delightful exclamation: **"WOW!"** David had great joy in pondering God's blessing promised to Abraham, ". . . in you all the families of the earth shall be blessed." Genesis 12:3. In his Bible he had underlined it with red and wrote next to it: "Key Promise." This promise is to the whole family of believing parents. Abraham believed God's covenant of blessing for his children and God was pleased. David believed that the God of Abraham kept His promise and sent the Savior to bless him and his family. To David it was always, "As for me and my house." The closing words of his letter again speak of his faith in the saving work of the Holy Spirit in the hearts of his children:

Remember at Pentecost when so many were saved and baptized? The promise [of the Holy Spirit] is to you and to <u>your children! Acts 2:39</u>.

[Again, there is the underline: "<u>Your children! Acts 2:39</u>"

In the New Testament Baptism took place in rivers. Our Baptism truly is in The River of Life or in The River Flowing From Emmanuel's Veins.

Love,
David

Jesus had given David this assurance when he was a young boy:

"Every one whom My Father gives Me will come to Me. I will never turn away anyone who comes to Me." John 6:37 TEV

Jesus never turned away anyone who came to Him, not even little children who were brought to Him. Now this devoted father would bring in baptism his baby Solomon Isaac to the same loving Savior and Lord of all. David, as head of his family, would publicly entrust his baby to Jesus for the faithful convicting work of the promised Holy Spirit. The prayer of the Lord Jesus at the Last Supper could be David's prayer:

> *"O Father! . . . And now I am coming to you; I am no longer in the world, but they are in the world.*
> *O holy Father! Keep them safe by the power of your name, the name you gave me, so they may be one just as you and I are one." John 17:11 TEV*

David's letter explains so well that God finds pleasure only in what His beloved Son does in our hearts and what He is continually willing to do when we ask Him. Joy is the treasure that David found by searching to understand God from His Word. By his joy in Jesus he is wiping my tears away. I am beginning to understand God's command:

> *"In everything give thanks; for this is the will of God for you in Christ Jesus." 1 Thessalonians 5:18*

Now I turn to the booklet on "Infant Baptism" by John Sartelle. This booklet again contains David's love for his children. The writer lists New Testament incidents where children were blessed because of the parents' faith in Jesus. This message is so timely for me just now as I ponder God's dealing with our son and the future of all our children. David marked with red the statements that were important to him and underlined this title with red:

<u>"The child was restored because of the parent</u>

The daughter of a Jewish official died and Jesus restored her life because the father came to Him for help. Matthew 9:18-26

A Canaanite woman begged Jesus to have mercy on her daughter who was possessed by a demon. Jesus was greatly pleased with this mother's faith and cured her daughter in a moment. Matthew 15:22-28

Jesus commanded the father of an epileptic boy: ***"Bring your son to me."*** Jesus commanded the demon to leave and the boy was instantly healed. Matthew 17:14-18

Jesus' heart was filled with compassion when he saw a widow in a funeral procession weeping over her dead son. He stopped her and said: ***"Don't cry!"*** And Jesus gave back the dead son alive to his mother! Luke 7:11-17

An official of the city of Capernaum rushed to Jesus to get help for his son who was near death. Jesus declared: ***"Go! Your son lives!"*** The father believed Jesus and his son was saved. John 4:46-53."

To this we can add the example of Zaccheus, who, in deep repentance, invited Jesus to his house. The Lord said to him:

> *"Today salvation has come to this house because he also is a son of Abraham."* Luke 19:9

The head of the family came to repentance, and Jesus received him and his whole family. God has a very special regard for the children of His people.

David's certainty of Acts 2:39, God's promise of the Holy Spirit to us parents concerning our children, reminds me of God's promise to us grandparents concerning our grandchildren:

> *"But the mercy of the Lord is from everlasting to everlasting on those who fear Him and His righteousness to <u>children's children,</u>*
> *To such as keep His covenant, and to those who remember His commandments to do them."* Psalm 103:17, 18 [underline added]

I remember that fearful morning, June 19, 1998, when an overwhelming evil terror startled me out of bed at 4:00 a.m. in the dark. I was overcome with despair by what the powers of darkness are doing in perverting America. I fell on my knees to plead with God for His mercy for my children and grandchildren who are surrounded with the sin-loving culture of our day. I pleaded with God to keep my loved ones holy and pure for Himself. It was on that same day in the evening when God unexpectedly took our David to Himself. Yet, the pain of this crushing blow is being replaced by the glad tidings of great joy that David left behind for me:

"Mom, remember, "The promise is for you and your children: Acts 2:39."

God has answered my cry for my children and grandchildren, and – wonder of wonders – of all people, it is David who is giving me this assurance! David is the one whose death caused me to look with fear into the future of the rest of our children. Yet now, it is David who is giving me the confidence that the Holy Spirit will keep them safe in our heavenly Father's loving plan. God's beloved Son proved to us that His Father is worthy of my unquestioning trust when He died for us on the cross. His Father kept His promise and raised Him from the dead and took Him back to glory to be the Sovereign Lord of all.

An age-old hymn comes to comfort me now. It is based on the first few verses of Isaiah chapter 43. God called our son "through the deep waters to go:"

> How firm a foundation, ye saints of the Lord,
> Is laid for your faith in His excellent Word!
> What more can He say than to you He hath said,
> To you who for refuge to Jesus have fled?
>
> Fear not, I am with thee. Oh, be not dismayed,
> For I am thy God, I will still give thee aid,
> I'll strengthen thee, help thee, and cause thee to stand,
> Upheld by My gracious omnipotent hand.
>
> When through the deep waters I call thee to go,
> The rivers of sorrow shall not overflow,

For I will be with thee, thy trials to bless,
And sanctify to thee thy deepest distress.

When through fiery trials thy pathway shall lie,
My grace all sufficient shall be thy supply,
The flame shall not hurt thee; I only design,
Thy dross to consume and thy gold to refine.

The soul that on Jesus hath leaned for repose,
I will not, I will not desert to his foes,
That soul, though all hell should endeavor to shake,
I'll never, no never, no never forsake!

American Melody from John Rippon's
Selection of Hymns, "K" 1787

The Pentecost Promise Is To Parents

Acts 2:39
"Remember at Pentecost when so many were saved and Baptized? "The promise is for you and your children"

David believed the Pentecost promise

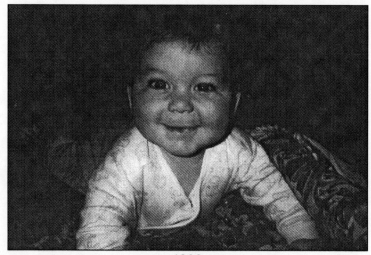

1999
Baby Solomon Isaac, one year old

The Bible David Left Behind

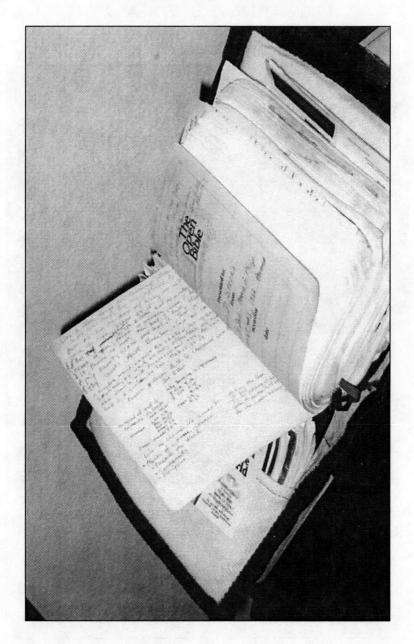

"Where Your Treasure Is,
There Will Your Heart Be Also"
Matthew 6:21

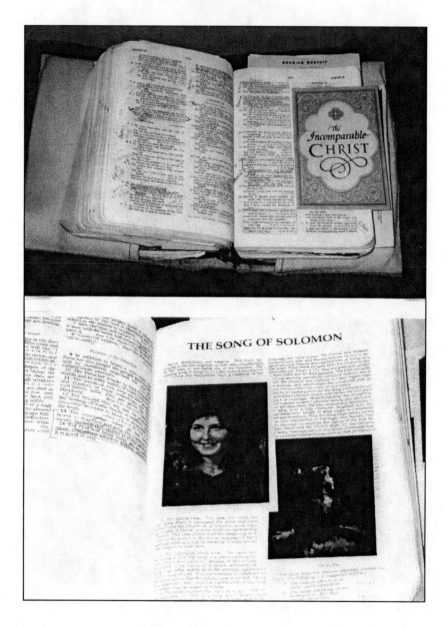

8

THE BIBLE THAT
DAVID LEFT BEHIND

It is a thrill for me to open David's well-used Bible. His many notations tell me that hisheart yearned to know God and to please Him. In response God expressed His pleasure to him by giving him many promises to make His Word a feast of His love to him.

Among David' s notations my attention is drawn to some passages next to which he wrote the word *"PRAYER,"* written with red ink and next to others the word *"PROMISE,"* also with red ink. Next to the passage marked *"PRAYER,"* there is a cross reference leading to the verse marked *"PROMISE,"* and next to that passage there is a cross-reference leading back to the verse marked *"PRAYER."*

Apparently, David had a unique way of reading his Bible. God's Word was his prayer-life. This was his own special way of marking in his Bible the prayers that he had prayed and the promises that God had given him in answer to his prayers.

Whenever he encountered a Bible passage that expressed the burden of his heart, he underlined it with red and wrote the word *"PRAYER"* next to it. As he went on studying his Bible, the Lord led him to a passage that was a direct answer to the verse that he had marked as his own prayer. Next to his prayer-verse he wrote the cross-reference of where he found God's answer to his prayer. As I look up that cross-reference I find it marked with red: *"PROMISE"* with David's note of the cross-reference that leads me back to his prayer-verse.

David had a deep longing to get to know God as the joy of his heart. In the book of Psalms he found the prayer that asks God for this joy for all of God's people. He marked it as his own prayer:

"PRAYER"

"Wilt Thou not Thyself revive us again, that Thy people may rejoice in Thee?" Psalm 85:6

God led him to His answer in Isaiah 57:15. He underlined it with red and marked it with the word:

"PROMISE"

"For thus says the high and exalted One
Who lives forever,
Whose name is Holy:
I dwell on the high and holy place,
And also with the contrite and lowly of spirit
In order to revive the spirit of the lowly,
And to revive the heart of the contrite."

"I dwell . . . with the contrite and lowly of spirit . . ." I see David's handwriting on the margin:

"In Jesus, the Exalted One lowered Himself to come and speak to us."

David's cross reference, "Psalm 85:6," shows that this is God's answer to his prayer for joy in God.

David had a burning desire to be God's servant. He had applied to several missions hoping for fruitful service somewhere overseas, but the final plans never did work out. It may have been a disappointment to him that—instead of spreading God's good news overseas—he was only able to live a very simple, ordinary life at home. It may have been at this time when he placed this handwritten note into his Bible: "I want to work on acceptance of weakness. I will choose a Scripture verse (2 Corinthians 12:9,10) to memorize and meditate on (Jeremiah 29:11-13), David Steers, PG." God knows the heart of those who are brokenhearted because of their failure to live up to His holy worthiness. How happy our son must have been to hear from God that He does not reject those who are of a lowly spirit, who admit that they are not capable of doing something great for God. On the contrary, the high and exalted One comes to live with them to revive them to a new life with His Presence within them. David found the joy of God in knowing that He had come to live within him even though he had nothing to offer to Him.

What can I say to the next **"PRAYER"** and **"PROMISE"** passages that I find in David's Bible? They fit right in with the very first quotation that David wrote on the fly leaf of his Bible:

"Like a deer longs for running streams, so my soul longs for You, my God. Psalm 42:1"

My heart overflows with wonder as I encounter this desire of David in a mysterious interchange between God and our son—request and God's answer. It fits most surprisingly the manner in which God took him to Himself by "immersion under water." This prayer and promise exchange is in John 4:14 and 15:

> *"Jesus said to the Samaritan woman: Whosoever drinks of the water that I shall give him shall never thirst, but the water that I shall give him, shall become in him a well of water springing up to eternal life."*

After these words David underlined the woman's request to Jesus and wrote next to it in red:

"PRAYER"

"Sir, give me this water that I thirst not . . ."

Next to the word *"PRAYER"* there is a cross reference, "Revelation 21:6." I turn to that reference and in the margin, next to the verse, there again is the word:

"PROMISE"

"It is done. I am the Alpha and the Omega, the begin-ning and the end. I will give to the one who thirsts from the spring of the water of life without cost."

David underlined this passage with red and wrote next to it the cross reference, "John 4:15," back to his *"PRAYER."*

I am overwhelmed! I realize that God did quench David's thirst for Him when He took our son to Himself. To have God Himself is better than any great attainment here on earth. The markings of the next pages in David's Bible truly show him as one of lowly spirit. David's Bible shows that he treasured God's mercy, the favor that He freely gives to those who admit that they could never earn it by their own efforts.

The first chapter of Luke in David's Bible is printed over two pages facing each other. David circled the word "mercy" in verses 58, 72 and 78 and connected them with a long line over the two open pages:

And her neighbors and her relatives heard that the Lord displayed His great
mercy
toward her and they were rejoicing." Luke 1:58

"To show
>   *mercy*
toward our fathers, and to remember His holy
covenant." Luke 1:72

"Because of the tender
>   *mercy*
of our God with which the Sunrise from on
high has visited us." Luke 1:78

On the bottom of this page David had written a note under Luke 2:10, 11:

"And the angel said to them, "Do not be afraid; for behold, I bring you good news of a great joy which shall be for all the people; for today in the city of David there has been born for you a Savior, who is Christ the Lord."

Under these words David wrote:

"We can have great joy in Jesus and we can bring that joy to others."

Truly, God did grant David's prayer that he might find his joy in God and that he could bring that joy to others. God's Book was his treasure, his own heart-to-heart talk with God. He found that the prayers written in the Bible put into words the needs of his own heart and that he could present these as his own to God. Then God led him to His promises and assured him that they are His direct, written answers to his prayers. David kept praying until he received the answer.

David liked to keep his important study notes, handwritten prayers and other reminders in the pockets of the cover that Leann had made for his Bible. The front pocket is packed full of pictures of missionary families for whom David and his loved ones prayed. Their family custom was to place a picture or a card from friends on the table at dinner. Before they gave thanks to God for the food, one of the children prayed for those people. All through his Bible David has reminders to think of others instead of himself.

Among other treasures that David packed into the pockets of his Bible cover is a booklet with the title "Global Prayer Digest," a daily prayer-guide "That All The Peoples Of The Earth May Know—1 Kings 8:60." The page is turned back where the title says, "Pray for the 40,000 Animist CUNAS of Panama." This refers to the Indian tribe of Valerio Lopez, David's friend whom he took to the Christian Service Men's Home while he served in the U. S. Army in Panama. Valerio became a Christian and now takes the "Jesus" film to show his people. David kept him in his prayers.

There are other treasures packed into the pocket of the cover. No wonder that at his church David was known as "The Man With The Round Bible." In the cover there is a bulletin from a Gideon dinner and one from the 1996 missions conference at Riveroaks Church entitled "No Toil For Jesus Shall Be In Vain." Also, there is a study on the Holy Spirit and a printed study of "The Westminster Confession of Faith, Chapter 12 Adoption," as well as his own handwritten study of the book of Haggai. Among the pages of the Bible there are leaflets "The Incomparable Christ," "The Sanctity Of Human Life" and a booklet "A Christ Without A Cross?" David counted these as his precious possessions.

In the cover and through the pages of the Bible there is evidence that David listened attentively to Pastor Spink's teaching. Each Sunday the outline of the pastor's sermon is in the bulletin with words left blank to be filled in during the message. . David not only filled in the words, but he also kept the teaching handy to remind him to live by them.

On the fly leaf of his Bible below his first quotation from Psalm 42:1, David wrote:

"But as for me and my house, we will serve the Lord. Joshua 24:15"

"Come Thou fount of every blessing, tune my heart to sing Thy grace.
Let Thy goodness, like a fetter, bind my

wandering heart to Thee;
Prone to wander, Lord, I feel it,
Prone to leave the God I love;
Here's my heart, O take and seal it; seal
it for Thy courts above. Amen "

"Therefore, since we have a kingdom
which cannot be shaken, let us show our
gratitude by which we may offer to God
our acceptable service with reverence and
awe, for our God is a consuming fire.
(Hebrews 12:28, 29)"

"Pursue degree A.U.G. (Approved Unto
God) Jim Elliot"

"Live your Christian life - Coram Deo –
Before the face of God ,
In the presence of God, Under the
authority of God. For the honor and glory
of God."

"He who now lives as our King, died to
be our Savior."

As I turn the pages in David's Bible, a shock awaits me. A church bulletin! I check the date and the wound bursts open in my heart. It is from the last Sunday that he attended church. The heading reads:

Pear Orchard Presbyterian Church,
Ridgeland, MS
Morning Worship, June 14, 1998 at 10:30 a.m.

Once again, my tears stream down. On that day, as our son walked into the church with his joyful smile and his "Round Bible," who would have thought that this would be his last Sunday worship on earth? Who would have thought that God had picked him to be the one to confirm the faithful pastor's warning to be ready for Jesus' unexpected return?

Next to the title page of The Song of Solomon there is a lovely photo of Leann. Also in the Bible there are photos of Christalyn and Benjamin. As I continue turning the pages there is another prayer-verse which shows how this loving father prayed for his children:

"PRAYER"

"O Lord, the God of our fathers, art Thou not God in the heavens? And art Thou not ruler over all the kingdoms of the nations?

Power and might are in Thy hand so that no one can stand against Thee." 2 Chronicles 20:6

Next to this verse David marked Genesis 17:7, as cross reference:

"PROMISE"

"And I will establish My covenant between Me and you and your descendants after you throughout their generations for an everlasting covenant, to be God to you and to your descendants after you."

This is the Old Testament promise that God fulfilled on Pentecost Sunday in the coming of the Holy Spirit, the promise which—in his last letter to me—David claimed for himself and for his children:

"Mom, . . . rejoice with us at the Baptism of Solomon Isaac and remember from Acts 2:39 "The promise of the Holy Spirit is to you and to your children.

The covenant God made with Abraham is EVERLASTING with him and all his descendants: See Genesis 17:7."

In his Bible next to Genesis 17:7 David wrote "Key Promise" and "2 Chronicles 20:6" leading us back to his prayer. Clearly, the promise of the Holy Spirit " . . . to you and <u>to your children</u> . . . " was given to David in answer to his fervent prayers for his children.

As I continue to turn the pages of his Bible once more my tears well up: David marked as his prayer a prayer for orphans! He did not know that he was praying for his own fatherless children:

"PRAYER"

"Vindicate the weak and the fatherless; do justice to the afflicted and destitute." Psalm 82:3

Next to this verse David put as cross-reference "Luke 4:18," where the Lord Jesus declares:

"PROMISE"

"THE SPIRIT OF THE LORD IS UPON ME,
BECAUSE HE ANOINTED ME TO PREACH
  THE GOSPEL TO THE POOR.
"He has sent me to heal the brokenhearted" NKJ

HE HAS SENT ME TO PROCLAIM RELEASE TO
  THE CAPTIVES,
AND RECOVERY OF SIGHT TO THE BLIND,
TO SET FREE THOSE WHO ARE DOWNTRODDEN,
TO PROCLAIM THE FAVORABLE YEAR OF
  THE LORD."

David's cross-reference, "Psalm 82:3" leads us back to his prayer. This daddy left his Bible behind, but he took with him the promises that God had made to him for his family. He is now standing in the presence of God our Father, at the feet of our Living Savior, presenting from God's own written Word the promises given him for his fatherless children.

There are many more *"PRAYER"* and *"PROMISE"*

markings. Here are some more samples:

"PRAYER"

"Acquit me of hidden faults." Psalm 19:12

"PROMISE"

"I shall give them one heart, and shall put a new spirit within them. And I shall take the heart of stone out of their flesh and give them a heart of flesh, that they may walk in My statutes and keep My ordinances, and do them. Then they will be My people, and I shall be their God." Ezekiel 11:19, 20

This answer is actually the New Covenant that our Lord Jesus left behind for us at the Last Supper, sealed with his own precious blood of the cross. Hearing this David must have come with great joy to the Lord's table to receive the bread and the wine, the tangible remembrances that Jesus is now bodily alive from the dead and that He is faithfully keeping His promises as Sovereign Lord of every heart. David kept on clinging to the Lord Jesus' New Covenant to save him from his sin:

"PRAYER"

"Remove the false way from me and graciously grant me Thy law." Psalm 119:29

"PROMISE"

"FOR THIS IS THE COVENANT THAT I WILL MAKE WITH THE HOUSE OF ISRAEL AFTER THOSE DAYS, SAYS THE LORD,
I WILL PUT MY LAWS INTO THEIR MINDS,
AND I WILL WRITE THEM UPON THEIR HEARTS.
AND I WILL BE THEIR GOD, AND THEY SHALL

BE MY PEOPLE." Hebrews 8:10

David never grew tired of seeking the Lord, who never failed to give him specific answers to his prayers:

"PRAYER"

"My eyes are toward Thee, O God the Lord, in Thee I take refuge, do not leave me defenseless. Psalm 141:8

"PROMISE"

"The Lord has regarded the prayer of the destitute and has not despised their prayer." Psalm 102:17

"PRAYER"

"With Thy counsel Thou wilt guide me, And afterward receive me to glory." Psalm 73:24

"PROMISE"

"For such is God,
Our God forever and ever;
He will be guide us until death." Psalm 48:14

Before David met Leann, he had experienced a very difficult time of testing. He was attacked by false accusations at his work His brother, Philip, and Philip's wife, Bonnie, wrote him a very special letter to strengthen him in the Lord. David kept this letter in his Bible next to Psalm 31, which we had prayed and prayed for him at the time. Again, there are red markings:

"In Thee, O LORD, I have taken refuge;
Let me never be ashamed;
In Thy righteousness deliver me . . .
For Thou art my rock and my fortress:

For Thy name's sake Thou wilt lead me and guide me.
Thou wilt pull me out of the net which they have
secretly laid for me . . .
I will rejoice and be glad in Thy loving-kindness,
Because Thou hast seen my affliction;
Thou hast known the troubles of my soul . . .
Let me not be put to shame, O LORD,
for I call upon Thee . . .
How great is Thy goodness, which Thou hast stored up
for those who fear Thee,
Which Thou hast wrought for those
who take refuge in Thee,
Before the sons of men!
Thou dost hide them in the secret place of
Thy presence from the conspiracies of man;
Thou dost keep them secretly in a shelter
from the strife of tongues."

Psalm:31:9

"PRAYER"

9 Be gracious to me, O LORD, for I am in
distress,   Ps. 69:14; 69:17
My eye is wasted away from grief, my
soul and my body also.   Ps. 6:7 Is 49:13

David's marking leads us to the promise in Isaiah 49:13:

"PROMISE"

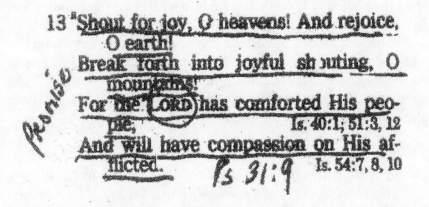

We asked David how he was facing the problem, he answered:

> " . . . *the cup which the Father has given Me, shall I not drink it?" John 18:11b*

I'll never forget a statement David made to me on his wedding day. In the course of a discussion that we had together he exclaimed, "Don't you know that Jesus opened up the new and living way for us into God's presence?" Through his diligent Bible study the heavenly Father revealed to him that our crucified, risen Lord Himself is our new and living way into His presence. He is the New Way that will forever stay open for us.

Phil and I are learning to praise God even though at times we hurt so much. As we study David's Bible we discover the messages of joy that he left behind for us. He is bringing us the joy that he found in Jesus. He is also teaching us how to make our prayers a delight to God, simply by learning from Scripture what kind of prayers He is eager to answer. Joy is the victory of our Lord Jesus in us, when we bow to His Father's will like He did.

June 24, 1998 - July 9, 1998

While we are in San Antonio waiting for the news of Baby Solomon's arrival I am gathering memories of David. I am assembling the photos of David's funeral into folders for our children and friends. When our daughters, Marion and Yolan, receive their folder, they call me to protest the choice of the photo that Philip had taken of David in his casket. "This photo is too painful for us to see," they claim. I must explain my special reason to them. "The photo clearly shows the words of Jesus' prayer on the paper that I placed next to David in the casket:

> *'Father, I will that all those whom You have given Me be with Me where I am, that they may see My glory, the glory which You have given Me—in Your great love to Me—before the foundation of the world. John 17:24'*

Jesus' prayer is the only reason why I am able to look at that photo of our precious David," I insist. "In that casket he is covered with the promises of the One who is now our risen Lord in glory. The words of His prayer have healing power in my heart." I think they understand.

Among the memories that David left behind, I also assemble some that I plan to show to Leann and the children. My favorites are the Mother's Day cards that David sent me. On one of them he added this extra note:

"Thank you, Mom, for raising me to love Jesus."

On another Mother's Day card David added "John 16:19-22" for me to look up. How timely Jesus' words are to me now:

> *"A little while and you shall see Me no more; again a little while and you will see Me . . .*
> *because I go to the Father . . .*

Truly, truly, I say to you, you will weep and lament . . .
But your sorrow will turn into joy . . .
I will see you again and your heart will rejoice, and no
one will take your joy from you."

Oh, how I cling to this precious promise of Jesus: "I will see you again!"

I will see Jesus and when I see Jesus, I will see David and all my other departed loved ones.

More Promises To David's Prayers

David Kept this cartoon in his Bible at Isaiah chapter 54, where he had found specific answers as promises to his prayers.

"PRAYER:" "O LORD, rebuke me not in Thy wrath: and chasten me not in Thy burning anger." (Psalm 38:1)

"PROMISE:" "For this is like the days of Noah to Me; when I swore that the waters of Noah should not flood the earth again, so I have sworn that I will not be angry with you." (Isaiah 54:9)

"PRAYER" "O LORD, why dost Thou reject me soul? Why doest Thou hide Thy face from me? (Psalm 88:14)

"PROMISE:" "I hid My face from you for a moment; but with everlasting lovingkindness I will have compassion on you, says the LORD, your Redeemer." (Isaiah 54:8)

"PRAYER" "Redeem me from the oppression of man, that I may keep Thy precepts." (Psalm 119:134)

"PROMISE:" "In righteousness you will be established: you will be far from oppression, for you will not fear, and from terror, for it will not come near you." (Isaiah 54:14)

"And all your children will be taught of the Lord." (Isaiah 54:13)

9

BABY SOLOMON ISAAC ARRIVES

Thursday, July 9, 1998

Phil and I receive the joyful news of the safe arrival of Baby Solomon Isaac. Mother and baby are well, thanks to the Lord. The baby, as a special gift from God, doesn't seem to suffer from the sudden shock his mother had to face before his birth.

At the Riveroaks Hospital, in Jackson, Leann's mom and dad, Christalyn, Benjamin and a neighbor lady were present at the baby's birth. We rejoice that, in the absence of her deeply caring husband, Leann was surrounded with her loving family and with kind, supportive people. The doctor was most reassuring, and Tammy, a well-trained labor and delivery coach, is Leann's friend from church.

Friday, July 10, 1998

On our way from San Antonio to Ridgeland to welcome the new baby, Phil and I stop for overnight in Baton Rouge We go from motel to motel in our search for a room, but there are no vacancies.

Finally, we have to settle in a motel that is not our first choice.

In the parking lot the Lord treats us to a most pleasant surprise. Phil exclaims, "Look! The Archers!" Yes! It is Leslie and Naomi Archer, our loving prayer partners, who had surprised us at our David's funeral. They "happen" to be on their way to Corpus Christi, while we are on our way in the opposite direction to Jackson. The Lord arranged for our paths to cross in Baton Rouge. We have a joyous time sharing news with one another and putting our arms around each other in heartfelt united prayer!

Saturday, July 11, 1998

Phil and I arrive at Leann's in time to have a quick visit with her parents before they must begin their long drive back to Indiana.

They are glad that we can take over helping Leann. Baby Solomon has jaundice and has to be taken to the doctor for a check-up. Grandpa offers to watch Christalyn and Benjamin so they can play at home, but they choose to come with us. They don't want to let their treasured newborn baby brother out of sight.

In the evening Christalyn reminds us of Isaiah 51, the wonderful words of life that she had read to us in Memphis. She reads it over several times to us:

> *"Awake, awake, put on strength,*
> *O arm of the Lord!*
> *Awake as in the ancient days,*
> *In the generations of old . . . .*
> *Are You not the One who dried up the sea,*
> *The waters of the great deep;*
> *That made the depth of the sea a road*
> *For the redeemed to cross over?*
> *So the ransomed of the Lord shall return,*
> *And come to Zion with singing,*
> *With everlasting joy on their heads,*
> *They shall obtain joy and gladness;*
> *Sorrow and sighing shall flee away."*
> *Isaiah 51:10,11*

Right now these words are still only a faint hope. It will take time for me to be able to truly accept them as a joyful reality in my soul. Here in the apartment we have vivid memories of David from our last visit. His radiant smile, from just a few weeks ago, is stamped in my heart.

So much joy and so much grief is mixed together. We rejoice over the darling baby boy, while our hearts weep in deep mourning over his missing daddy. As we take the precious baby into our arms we remember how his daddy was looking forward with joy to holding him in his arms like this. Even before the baby's birth he loved him so much, but he will never hug him in his arms in this life. A prayer of desperate confession wells up within me:

> Father, forgive me! Here I am again all broken up about Your dealings with me. One minute I am full of faith, while the next minute I am ready to fall apart.
>
> Father, Your Word tells us that You sent Your Son to heal the brokenhearted. You see my heart.
>
> How can I know Your love now when I hurt so much? You have taken away the father of our darling Baby Solomon. You have taken him away so suddenly, so unexpectedly, so publicly, just at the time when his family needs him most.

To find comfort Leann takes the family hymn book from the bookshelf. We invite the children to join us in the song:

> Oh, how He loves you and me,
> Oh, how He loves you and me,
> He gave His life, What more could He give,
> Oh, how He loves you and me.
>
> Oh, how He loves you and me,
> Jesus to Calv'ry did go, His love for mankind to show,
> What He did there brought hope from despair.
> Oh, how He loves you and me!

We keep singing this song over and over, trusting God to make His precious glad tidings of good news a reality in our hearts.

Christalyn   Baby Solomon   Benjamin

Fall of 1998

10

GOD HAS SURPRISES
FOR THE WIDOW

Tuesday, July 14, 1998

Thank God Grandpa Steers is a man of action. He can't leave Leann here in this apartment where every memory will tear at her heart. He has to find another place for her to live.

We turn to God in fervent prayer for His leading in this important step toward the future of Leann and her children. Her desire is to move back to Memphis, back to the church home where she and David had attended for nine years.

Leann has a close friend, Paula, who is a real estate agent in Memphis. Grandpa and Paula spend today searching for an apartment that would best suit Leann's abruptly changed situation. But the prospects are disappointing, since there are very few places within an affordable price range. After much searching, finally, Grandpa and Paula find a pleasant apartment in a nice apartment complex and make the down payment.

In the evening Paula calls Leann to report on the apartment hunt, "Your father-in-law is a man on a mission! He's 82 years old, but he wore me out! We found a great place for you!"

Grandpa also has a report on his visit to Memphis: "I went to David's grave for a time of prayer. God gave me hope in a very special way. He sent a beautiful butterfly to flutter around above the grave all during the time I was praying. That beautiful butterfly started out like an ugly worm-cocoon. That makes me think of David's body buried in the ground. But as I watched it flying back and forth, I was seeing a miracle. It is out of an ugly worm-cocoon that God made that beautiful butterfly. God will make a new creation out of David's body, too, when He raises him to new life in the resurrection."

Soon the deacons of Pear Orchard Church hear the news that there is an apartment in Memphis ready for Leann. They arrange for a truck and offer to move all her belongings on July 29. The deacons of Riveroaks Church promise to complete the unloading at the Memphis apartment. God is providing wonderfully.

Wednesday, July 15, 1998

Today our family is to attend the baby shower that the ladies of Leann's church and the neighbor ladies in her apartment complex organized for her. The superintendent of the apartment complex invited them to arrange their celebration at the club house.

As we arrive, a friendly lady welcomes us and then accompanies us as we proceed toward the wide entrance into the impressive, beautiful living room. At the doorway I stop with a jolt. I can't take another step. Across the room, facing me, is a large picture window in full view of the swimming pool where David had spent his last evening with his family. The sight hit me like a heavy blow, and I can't go on.

The pool can't be seen from the street or from Leann's apartment. But now I can't avoid seeing it. I was hoping that I would never to have to see it at all.

"Oh! The pool!" I gasp. It is so small! How can this be where our son, the expert swimmer, drowned? Can this be where he took his last breath? How could our David have lost his life in such a small pool? My grief is overtakes me and I sink into the depth of despair. I don't think I can go any further without breaking down in bitter tears.

The room is full of happy, smiling ladies, but I am doing all I can to fight back my tears. They have gone out of their way to arrange this festive gathering to help us rejoice over our Baby Solomon and to help us find comfort for our great sorrow. I would so much like to express my gratitude, but I am torn up with inner emotions. That troubling thought of our David's last breath brings to my mind how in his Bible David had underlined with red this awe-inspiring description of our God:

> "*. . . the Most High God is ruler over the realm of mankind, . . . the Lord of heaven. . . the God in whose hand are your life-breath and your ways* . . ." Daniel 5:21c, 22ac

Almost on every page of his Bible David had circled with red the names of God. He also circled the adjective "awesome" whenever it appears to describe God. Should it surprise me that the Most High God, our Creator, has the right to our son's breath and to all his ways?

Thankfully, all the ladies are busy greeting Leann and admiring the baby. I don't need to talk to anyone for now. I whisper, "Lord Jesus! I need You! My heart cries, "The sight of that pool is torturing me. Am I the only one with this unspeakable heartache?"

There is another older lady, a retired pastor's wife, sitting on a secluded couch. I sink down beside her. There is compassion in her eyes. She knows I am David's mother, and she senses my inner struggle. She also has gone through the pain of having to bury a loved one. But the Lord Jesus has done a miracle in her heart. He has given her that peace beyond understanding that He has for all those who go to Him for consolation.

She turns to me to explain: "Through the reading of Isaiah chapter 43 the Lord made Himself known to me in a new way. He showed me that He Himself charted out my path and my loved one's path, even before He created us. To Him there are no surprises, no accidents. From His Word He showed me how He is bringing good out of my sorrow. He will show you, too, His purpose, even through your tears and trials. He will assure you that He always and unfailingly only has good for us all in His plan."

How gracious our Lord is to lead me to this mature Christian lady who was able to give me the right words at the right time! I determine to look up Isaiah 43 in David's Bible as soon as I return to the apartment.

The lovely presents for the baby are passed around, to include us all with Leann in the enjoyment of the celebration. I hear muffled whisperings about a big surprise that is kept for the end. The ladies joined together to buy it for Leann, knowing that she could not afford it for herself. Finally, there is a hush, and the ladies bring out a beautifully woven, big white wicker rocking chair. It is just for Leann, just the kind she has dreamed of having for a long time.

How lovingly the Lord is providing for Leann in bringing such thoughtful and compassionate friends into her life just now. She needed this assurance of God's love to her right now!

**Leann and Baby Solomon enjoy the
beautiful rocking chair given them
by the ladies at the baby shower.**

God is love and love is from God in every heart, even in the
ones who do not know Him. It is God's love that brought together
these ladies from the apartment complex and from the church to
express loving compassion to a newly widowed mother. God is
always working to build His family.

Back at the apartment I quickly look up Isaiah 43 in David's
Bible. What exactly are the words that brought comfort to the lady
who spoke to me so kindly at the baby shower?

As I open the page, I can hardly contain myself. What a blessed
surprise is waiting for me there! Starting with the first ones many of
the verses are marked up with David's red pen! Our almighty and
all-knowing heavenly Father spoke to our son of His love to him in
order to prepare him for this unusual plan that He had for him:

> *"But now, <u>thus says the Lord, Your Creator . . .</u>*
> *<u>He who formed you</u> . . .*
> *<u>Do not fear, for I have redeemed you;</u>*
> *<u>I have called you by name: you are Mine!</u>*
> *When you pass through the waters, I will*
> *be with you . . .*
> *for <u>I am the Lord your God,</u>*
> *<u>the Holy One of Israel, your Savior . . .</u>*
> *. . . you are <u>precious</u> in My sight,*
> *since you are <u>honored</u> and <u>I love you</u> . . . .*
> *<u>Do not fear, for I am with you . . ."</u>*
> *Isaiah 43:1-5*

> *<u>"I am the Lord, your Holy One,</u>*
> *<u>The Creator of Israel, your King . . .</u>*
> *<u>. . . Behold, I will do something new . . ."</u>*
> *Isaiah 43:15, 19*

How fitting! How right for David! Our wonderful God had
lavished our son with His love and words of assurance. He speaks
to me, too, through the markings that David left behind in his Bible!

Then I notice that David marked a cross-reference next to verse
4: "Zephaniah 3:17"

Turning to it I find verses 14 and 15 underlined:

> *"Shout in triumph, O Israel! . . .*
> *Rejoice and exalt with all your heart . . .*
> *The Lord has taken away His judgment against you,*
> *He has cleared away your enemies.*
> *The King of Israel, the Lord, is in your midst;*
> *You will fear disaster no more . . .*
>
> *"Do not be afraid, O Zion . . .*
> *The Lord your God is in your midst,*
> *A victorious warrior.*
> *He will exalt over you with joy,*
> *He will be quiet in His love;*
> *He will exalt over you with shouts of joy.*
> *He will renew you in His love; NKJ*
> *He will exalt over you with shouts of joy."*

David added at the end: "Singing," and the cross-reference back to "Isaiah 43:1-4."

What marvelously appropriate words! No wonder David was always so joyful, so secure in God, his Savior! What God had done to David is part of His great, wise plan for him and for us all. God makes no mistakes. He will never let us be disappointed in Him.

After we return from the baby shower Christalyn asks permission to go back to the club house. She has an idea. She needs a balloon for that idea. It has to be a balloon that can fly up. Her face looks forlorn when she returns. The ladies had already cleaned up after the party. The balloons have been taken away.

"Maybe Mrs. Robin has a balloon," Christalyn says. "May I go over to her house to ask?" But again she returns looking dejected. There are no balloons left. Christalyn is not about to give up. She must have a balloon!

"Christalyn," we ask, "why do you need a balloon so urgently?" She pulls out from her pocket a letter she had written, a letter to her daddy. This precious little girl wanted to use a balloon to send her love up to her daddy, asking him to send an answer.

We sit down to talk about it. We make a suggestion to Christalyn on how to reach her daddy: "You can ask the Lord Jesus to take your message to your daddy. Jesus is our only contact with heaven now."

As we talk, a new idea comes to us. We could find out from the Bible what Christalyn's daddy is doing in heaven, his new home. This will be a good subject for future Bible study, but right now the family has to get ready for the big move. While Leann and Grandma Steers take care of the household, Grandpa Steers is packing the belongings. Each day a few more boxes are added to the pile. The slowest part is the packing of the books. Leann and David love good books. They have a collection of classical and Christian books, some no longer in print.

This part of the packing proceeds slowly because Grandpa constantly finds some great book that he has to read first before packing it away. He notices one by Dr. Henry M. Morris entitled, "The Remarkable Record of Job." Dr. Morris is the founder of "The Institute for Creation Research," a ministry whose purpose is to present the truth that God is the Creator of our world. The book of Job, believed to be the oldest book of the Bible, has always fascinated Grandpa. He finds that Dr. Morris' study of Job presents the best defenses concerning the truth of God's creation.

Grandpa expected the book to be one of scientific explanations, but to his pleasant surprise Dr. Morris' words are not merely scientific. There, tucked away on page 93, Grandpa finds a most personal treasure—a ray of light in the darkness of this sorrow—for his father-heart that is still in deep mourning over the loss of his son, David. It is the answer to our puzzle as we are wondering what Christalyn's daddy might be doing in heaven now.

Dr. Morris explains Job's ordeal in the light of the New Testament's teaching in Ephesians 3:9-11 that God, the Father created our world by His Son, the Lord Jesus Christ, according to the eternal purpose to display the glory of His beloved Son. Beyond what our eyes can see He also created unseen beings above those which our human understanding can comprehend. The Church, God's family is to be used of God to make known the riches of His wisdom to the unseen beings, among these to Satan and also, to every human being. Dr. Morris writes:

Thus, Job's ordeal, and his faithfulness through it, was a marvelous testimony—not only to Satan but also to the entire host of heaven—of the glorious effectiveness of God's great plan. It provided tremendous incentive to all the holy angels to serve more faithfully themselves as "ministering spirits" to "the heirs of salvation."

The angels continue to this day observing with intense interest the out-workings of God's great salvation in our own lives, especially in times of stress and trouble.

"Of which salvation . . . the angels desire to look into." 1 Peter 1:10-12

<u>Our loved ones who already have gone from</u> this life <u>to be with the Lord also are probably deeply</u> concerned <u>observers of our lives on earth.</u> (Emphasis added.)

"Wherefore, seeing we also are compassed about with so great a cloud of witnesses . . .let us run with patience the race that is set before us, looking unto Jesus, the author and finisher of our faith; who for the joy that was set before him endured the cross, despising the shame, and is set down at the right hand of the throne of God." Hebrews 12:1,2

This study of the book of Job is a thrilling message that David left behind for his dad in his library. With glowing face Grandpa brings this explanation to the family: "Dr. Morris gives us a vision of heaven and it is a wonderful and glorious one. The book of Job tells us of a high balcony in heaven from where the heavenly beings can watch our heavenly Father, how He is working on earth to carry out His promises in our lives. This means that David is now joining the angels watching us down here. This is an answer to Christalyn who wanted to send a letter to her daddy."

Turning to the children Grandpa adds with a smile, "Christalyn, Benjamin and even Baby Solomon, you can be happy to know that your daddy's eyes are focused on what Jesus is doing in your lives."

The great interest of the heavenly beings in Job's faith in God in the midst of his test, is a comfort to us down here on earth. The concluding chapters of Job testify of God's wonderful, continual, providential and eternal care for all that He has created.

The book of Job brings to mind other Bible passages that show the intense interest of heavenly beings in our lives down here on earth. For instance,

> *"Jesus told them . . .*
> *In the same way, I tell you, there is joy in the presence of*
> *the angels of God over one sinner who repents." Luke 15:10*

> *". . . those who are considered worthy to attain . . .*
> *the resurrection from the dead are like angels, and are*
> *sons of God, being sons of the resurrection. Luke 20:36*

Our son David is enjoying eternity now on the heavenly Mount Zion, in the heavenly Jerusalem with Jesus, the Firstborn, and His Church, who are registered in heaven, and with the innumerable company of angels and "the spirits of just men made perfect." Hebrews 12:22-24. David loved being with Jesus. He knew Him as the Firstborn, the Mediator of the new and everlasting covenant that God had made with him and with his family. The next wonderful truth is a reality to him now:

> *". . . you were dead . . . but God . . . raised us up with*
> *Him (Christ) and seated us with Him in the heavenly*
> *places, in Christ Jesus,*
> *in order that in the ages to come He might show the*
> *surpassing riches of His grace in His kindness toward us*
> *in Christ Jesus. "Ephesians 2:6,7*

Even now, as we mourn our temporary loss of David, I can keep telling our grandchildren, whenever we see a rainbow, "God will always be kind to us!" The day will come when our sorrow will turn into joy, when we will fully understand

> *" . . . the surpassing riches of His grace in His*
> *kindness toward us in Christ Jesus."*

Monday, July 20, 1998

A call comes from the Memphis apartment complex: "We need more information from Mr. Steers and Leann." It is a time-consuming process to secure all sorts of information from agencies, especially because Phil has to keep contacting San Antonio. Leann, too, has to provide more references, some from out of town. The week passes with daily phone and fax dispatches between Leann's apartment and the superintendent of the Memphis apartment complex. Each time the calls are more and more unfriendly and demanding, and the prospect of the move to Memphis becomes more and more unpleasant.

Thursday, July 23, 1998

Phil and I have an unforgettable meeting with Pastor Carl Kalberkamp in his office at Pear Orchard Presbyterian Church. He is the pastor who was in the midst of preaching a series of Sunday sermons warning his congregation of Jesus' unexpected coming, when God suddenly called David home. God used our son to confirm this faithful pastor's warnings to his congregation in a frightful manner, and he deeply shares the sentiments of our tearful mourning with us.

The pastor has prepared himself—with much prayer and searching of Scripture—to strengthen us in the Lord during our deep sorrow. He admonishes us:

" Rejoice in hope. Our hope is in God, not in the way our circumstances work out. No matter what the testing, our relationship to God does not change. He is our hope and joy!

"Look at the example of Job. God's love for Job was more powerful than anything Satan could do to him. After his testing was accomplished, Job exclaimed in his prayer with joy to God,
'I have heard of You by the hearing of the ear, but now my eyes see You.' Job 42:5

"God works in all our experiences in such a way that we can know Him more and more clearly and depend on Him more and more fully.

"Joy comes in prayer. God promised:

'I will make you joyful in My house of prayer.'
Isaiah 56:7

"So, turn to God in prayer! Offer to God the sacrifice of joy! Leann and the children are no less in the hand of God now, without David, than they were with David. God has a great plan for Leann, Christalyn, Benjamin and Baby Solomon. Her children still have a Father: God, the Father.

"We are on a train. God is the Engineer. He has switched us to a new track to move us forward in His mercy into a fuller knowledge of Him. The Lord Jesus made His purpose known with these words:

. . . I will build My church, My family, and the gates of
hell shall not prevail against My family.

When God is testing our faith we have a choice either to respond to Him in rebellion or in fuller dependence on Him!"

This is a challenge and it makes me face a choice. I accept the challenge. I choose dependence, not rebellion. I feel and know that at this moment I have made a decision to become obedient to God no matter what the cost. This is a turning point that will affect all my life. God stamps His approval on my resolve as I express it in the hearing of the pastor and my husband. We unite our hearts in prayer and truly God is assuring me that He heard us. His answer is certain.

Thank you, Pastor Kalberkamp, for your unhurried, truly compassionate words with us. Thank you for your understanding of our tears.

Monday, July 27, 1998

Another call comes from the Memphis apartment complex. This

is the fourth person to contact us for more information. And not only that! Now they want a $3000 advance deposit for the rent! Apparently they have had second thoughts about renting to a husbandless mother of three children with an 82-year-old father- in-law promising to make the payments for them. They have made our dealings with them impossible! Leann has no choice. She cancels her plans to move to that apartment complex.

Now what will become of the arrangements that the deacons of Pear Orchard Church and the deacons of Riveroaks Church have worked out for the move on July 29? All the men have arranged for leave from work in order to help Leann make the move in one morning.

Furthermore, Leann has already terminated her contract with the owners of her present apartment. Where will she go? Everything in Leann's apartment is packed into boxes waiting for the move. The ladies of Pear Orchard Church have been furnishing the meals because Leann has packed away everything that belongs in her kitchen. Leann contacts Paula, her real estate agent friend, to see if she can find another apartment in a hurry in Memphis. But she receives the disappointing answer, "I can't find anything affordable!"

We are helpless. What are we to do? We can't leave Leann in this apartment surrounded with memories that are an agony to her. Many prayers go up for help in this unforeseen complication, but by evening there is no answer from God.

Tuesday, July 28, 1998, 8:00 AM

Leann takes her car for an oil change. As she waits, she picks up a torn part of a newspaper, the "For Rent" section. She rushes home to report, "There is a house for rent with a large yard," she tells Grandpa with excitement. "The price is affordable, and it's very close to Pear Orchard Church!"

Leann and Grandpa hurry over to see the house. How much better a house with a yard would be than a small place in an apartment complex! The owner "happens" to be there.

It is a nice house in a fine neighborhood with a fenced-in yard, but inside, especially the kitchen, is a dirty mess! The former renters had walked out without notice. The owner agrees to rent it out to Leann with a discount on the deposit if she is willing to clean it up herself. It's a deal! Leann signs the contract. Praise God! Leann now sees by this unexpected provision that the Lord is keeping her in Jackson, instead of letting her move to Memphis.

Immediately we get busy with the cleaning. The former renters left the refrigerator behind. Pastor Presley arranges to have it fixed. He keeps coming back to check if there is anything we need. The ladies of the church continue to provide generous meals.

Wednesday, July 29, 1998

The deacons of Pear Orchard Church and Pastor Presley arrive at Leann's apartment, as promised, early in the morning. They exchange jokes and smiles as they move all her belongings into the truck. Then, as they unload, they tease Leann, "Where are the deacons of the Memphis Church? They were supposed to be doing this!"

Their cheerful attitude makes the move very pleasant. They complete it by early afternoon. The families of the church have taken Christalyn and Benjamin to play with their children for the day. Amazingly, Leann is full of energy, even though she is caring day and night for her newborn.

In His grace, our Lord is keeping Leann busy, helping her to leave behind the past so she can look into the future for her precious children. The Lord is providing His promised enabling grace for this dear widowed mother, according to the words He spoke at the tomb of Lazarus:

If you believe Me, you shall see the glory of God.
John 11:40 (my own wording)

It is out of death that God creates resurrection life.

11

BABY SOLOMON IS BAPTIZED

Sunday, October 18, 1998, Memphis, TN

Today the Riveroaks Reformed Presbyterian Church family has a special celebration for Baby Solomon Isaac Steers. In his last letter to us, not knowing that it would be his last will, his daddy presented his decision that his expected baby son receive the sacrament of baptism. In his great love for his family he had prepared himself with wholehearted dedication to offer up his baby publicly to the heavenly Father in the name of our Lord Jesus Christ.

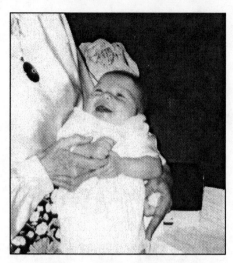

**Three months old Baby
Solomon is "All Smiles" at
his baptism.**

His daddy had planned to claim in the presence of the congregation the specific promises that God had given him concerning this child and his whole family. Today, we, his grandparents have gathered together with Leann and the children to carry out our son's last will.

All during the morning worship Baby Solomon rests happily in his Grandma's arms. When the time comes for his baptism, he is brought forward by his mother, Leann, and accompanied by Christalyn, Benjamin, and his Grandpa and Grandma Steers.

As Pastor Spink takes him into his arms to pray over him and to baptize him, Baby Solomon appears to be radiating the favor of heaven shining down on him. He is full of smiles, even when the cold water is applied to his forehead. His middle name "Isaac" means "Laughter." He is the "smilingest" baby we have ever seen.

In his last letter his daddy wrote of how he prayed that I could "rejoice with him and Leann at the baptism of Solomon Isaac." I am sure that he expected to bring his baby son in his own arms to present him to the Lord. This daddy's one aim in life was to have the heavenly Father's approval resting on his family. This blessing could only be realized by "family obedience." Baby Solomon must be included in this blessing. It was David's conviction that baptism is the first step of obedience in the life of faith. At his baby son's baptismal he would express publicly his assurance that the same gracious Lord who had received him when he himself was a young boy, would also receive his Baby Solomon as His own precious treasure. In the presence of the congregation he would entrust his baby to the same loving Lord who had taught him to love and obey His Word.

While he was still alive, Solomon's daddy taught God's Word to his family and reminded them often: "You have to be all for Jesus, or you are not for Jesus at all," Now David, this loving father, can be rejoicing in heaven with us down here according to the words that he had left behind:

We must obey God!
And so be blessed!
As for me and my house we will
be Baptised and serve the LORD!

"We will . . . be baptized and serve the Lord." David wanted God to be the Supreme Ruler of his family. This desire is evident from the prayer that he had marked with red in his Bible:

"PRAYER"

"O Lord God of our fathers, are You not God in heaven, and do You not rule over all the kingdoms of the nations, and in Your hand is there not power and might so that no one is able to withstand You?" 2 Chronicles 20:6

This is the supplication next to which David had marked "Genesis 17:7" as God's answer to his prayer for his children: The God of Abraham would be his God and his children's God forever:

"PROMISE"

"And I will establish My covenant between Me and you and your descendants after you in their generations, for an everlasting covenant, to be God to you and to your descendants after you."

Then, from the book of Acts David discovered with great joy that God did fulfill this promise at Pentecost when He gave the world the gift of the Holy Spirit. He is God's proof to us that Jesus did pay for our sins on the cross according to the Scriptures and that He did return to His glory with the Father, according to the Scriptures. David held on to his assurance that God has come to him in the same way as He has come to His people at Pentecost. God did this by giving him the gift of the Holy Spirit. It is this confidence that prompted David to write his emphatic words to me in his last letter:

Remember, Mom, from Acts 2:39:
"For the promise of the Holy Spirit is to you and to <u>your children..</u>"

This is the promise that brought David and Leann to the decision to offer their Baby Solomon to God in baptism. Yes! I give thanks unceasingly to our Father for the gift of the Holy Spirit, His greatest gift to us. Our Lord Jesus Himself tells us to ask and to receive this Gift from His Father:

"If you then, being evil, know how to give good gifts to your children, how much more will your heavenly Father give the Holy Spirit to those who ask Him." Luke 11:13

In his last letter David had explained so well that it is not the water that baptizes, but it is the Lord Jesus Himself who baptizes. He baptizes us with more than water. He immerses into His Holy Spirit all those who ask Him. David's desire was for God's blessing on his every activity.

Among his papers we found a sheet on which he was calculating the family budget at a time when he really struggled to make ends meet. On top of the sheet, before he started to list his expenses, he wrote this Scripture promise:

Malachi 3:10 "Bring the whole tithe into the Storehouse, so that there may be food in my house and test Me now in this" Says the Lord of Hosts, "if I will not open for you the windows o f heaven, and pour out for you a blessing until there is no more need

He underlined "test Me" and circled "you." David had accepted the challenge to entrust to God his tithes even when giving them could have appeared like a loss, rather than a gain.

But David had entrusted more than his tithes to God. He had entrusted himself fully to God. And his last letter shows that he had entrusted his whole family, his most precious treasure on earth, into the eternal safekeeping of our faithful God, the God of the Bible.

As mother and grandmother my treasures on earth are my children and grandchildren. I take to heart God's promise to those who entrust their treasures to Him, the promise that David had claimed:

> "... I will ... open for you the windows of heaven,
> and pour out for you a blessing until it overflows."
> *Malachi 3:10b*

As I watch Baby Solomon being baptized, I am of one accord with his daddy and mommy and join them in entrusting this precious baby boy to our Savior. And in my heart I entrust not only him, but also all our children and grandchildren to our Lord Jesus, who never turns away anyone who comes to Him:

"Then little children were brought to Him that He might put His hands on them and pray, but the disciples rebuked them.
But Jesus said: 'Let the little children come to Me and do not forbid them; for of such is the kingdom of heaven.'
And He laid His hands on them . . . "Matthew 19:13-15a NKJ

"And He took them up into His arms, laid His hands on them and blessed them." Mark 10:16

"Whoever receives this child in My name receives Me, and whoever receives Me receives Him who sent Me." Luke 9:48

From our experience with David I know now that God's promised abundant blessing does not mean a tearless life here on earth. But it does mean the future joys of heaven that are dearest to my heart:

"For what is our hope, or joy, or crown of rejoicing? Is it not even you [our children] in the presence of our Lord Jesus Christ at His coming?
For you are our glory and joy." 1 Thessalonians 2:19, 20 NKJ

With Baby Solomon in his arms Pastor Spink assures us that our God will never fail to keep His promises that He has given us in writing in his Holy Word, our Bible.

After the pastor's morning message, entitled "He Who Promised Is Faithful," the Sunday worship closes with this great hymn:

"Great is Thy faithfulness, O God my Father,
There is no shadow of turning with Thee.
Thou changest not; Thy compassions they fail not;
As Thou hast been, Thou forever wilt be . . . "

Yes! We are certain this is so!

Our faithful God did cause the desire and prayer of David's heart to be fulfilled:

> *"I hope and pray that you will under-stand Leann and me in our point of view and be able to rejoice with us at the Baptism of Solomon Isaac."*

Our God works miracles of understanding in human hearts.

After the service and his baptism Baby Solomon has a radiant smile for the many loving people who come to greet him. How wonderfully the Lord has blessed Leann, Christalyn and Benjamin with this new family member whom his daddy had left behind for them and for our family to love.

Once again we are filled with thanksgiving to our Lord who has blessed us at our worship with the Riveroaks Church family by granting us joyful unity of heart that He alone can give.

12

THE FIRST ANNIVERSARY AT DAVID'S GRAVE

Saturday, June 19, 1999

Today is the first anniversary of our David's homegoing. Leann, Christalyn, Benjamin and Baby Solomon meet with Grandpa and Grandma Steers in the beautiful Memory Hills Garden in Memphis, to join our hearts in a time of prayer at our loved one's graveside.

The children can't be still for very long. Soon they run around happily in the sparkling sunshine on the field of soft grass and beautiful wild flowers, unaware of the seriousness of what has happened in their lives. They delight in God's marvelous handiwork instead of staying at their father's grave. Leann is teaching them diligently to look to Jesus and to receive the comfort that He gives to them. They are taking their mother's teaching to heart. We adults lead our children by our example. As we accept the consolation offered to us in the Bible, we parents are the evidence to our children of the accuracy, the integrity, the infallibility, the completeness and relevance of God's holy Word.

The sight of our David's grave, again, brings before me the dreadful reality of this curse, death, and again the healing wounds of my heart are reopened. I feel unable to act on Pastor Kalberkamp's unforgettable challenge from God's Word: "Offer to God the sacrifice of joy! You have a choice. You can respond to God in dependence or in rebellion. You can rest on God's Word or continue in torment."

My naturally rebellious heart would rather hold on to my grief and blindly focus on my misery here at the grave of my son. But God's promise stands:

> *"I will make you joyful in My house of prayer."*
> Isaiah 56:7

This choice is too difficult for my grief so I ask God for a miracle in my heart. I ask Him to set me free from my self-centered, stubborn attitude so I can obey Him. I offer to God the sacrifice of joy and thanksgiving in spite of the struggle for the contrary within me. I have to listen to the last words that David wrote to me:

"We must obey God! And so be blessed!"

Is it really possible to celebrate and praise God while my heart is breaking here at the grave of our loved one?

Yes! Even though I can't stop my tears from flowing in deep mourning over my temporary loss of our precious David, I can cling to Jesus and His eternal good news of the future resurrection of our body:

> *" . . . I declare to you the gospel which I preached to you, which also you received and in which you stand, by which also you are saved, if you hold fast that word which I preached to you . . .*
> *that Christ died for our sins according to the*

*Scriptures, and that He was buried, and that He rose
again the third day according to the Scriptures, and that
He was seen by Cephas, then by the twelve.*

*After that He was seen by over five hundred brethren
at once . . .*

*After that He was seen by James, then by all the
apostles.*

Then last of all He was seen by me also . . ."

I Corinthians 15:1-8 NKJ

Here at the grave of my son I must remember that Jesus, God's
Son, also was dead and buried. But He rose from among the dead as
it was foretold in the Bible. Then He appeared to many of His disciples and convinced them that He is alive and would remain so
forever. He saves me and makes me His disciple as I believe this
good news. Even here, in my grief, our Lord Jesus Christ is worthy
of all praise for His glad tidings of great joy that will never change:

*"Behold, He is coming with clouds, and every eye will
see Him, even they who pierced Him . . . " Revelation 1:7*

*"When He is revealed, we shall be like Him, for we
shall see Him as He is." 1 John 3:2c*

Leann, in her beautiful solo voice, leads our family in singing:

"Praise God from whom all blessings flow,
`Praise Him all creatures here below,
Praise Him above ye heavenly hosts,
Praise Father, Son and Holy Ghost."

Leann asked us to sing this hymn because at the third line she
sees in her heart her beloved David at the throne of God. She knows
that he is praising God, and she joins her voice to his praises.

*"I will extol You, O Lord, for You have lifted me up,
and have not let my foes rejoice over me.*

O Lord my God, I cried out to You and You healed me . . .

You have turned for me my mourning into dancing, You have put off my sackcloth and clothed me with gladness,

To the end that my glory may sing praise to You and not be silent.

O Lord my God, I will give thanks to You forever."
Psalm 30:1, 11, 12 NKJ

Nothing compares to the promises we have in Jesus!

13

TRULY, JESUS HEALS THE BROKENHEARTED

January 2002

More than three years have passed since that dreadful moment when the tragic news of our David's unexpected death broke my heart. In my grief over the loss of our son, I am more than ever grateful that I could face this devastating blow to our family with the insights that God has given me from His written Word. Through the confusion of the ups and downs of this sorrowful circumstance God has given me a deeper understanding of this treasure that I have in my heart:

> *If you love Me, you will love and obey My Word and My Father will love you and My Father and I will come to you and make Our home with you.* [This is what John 14:23 says to me]

God has come to live within me. I did not choose Him but He chose me and He has taken possession of me. I am His and He is mine forever. There is no earthly circumstance that can take my God away from me. Through the death of our son David, God showed me the awesome magnitude of this curse that afflicts mankind: Death! But, also, in the terrifying, changeless reality of our son's death my heavenly Father has revealed to me the glory of His Son. He sent Jesus to earth to give me, and to give us, out of His sacrificial death, His eternal life. Truly, Jesus fills me with wonder and worship. To think that He died on the cross for my sin and the sin of the world in order to give me and to give us this new life in God! He is able to give His eternal life because the heavenly Father raised Him from death to new life. He is alive in heaven. He is life, and not even death can destroy His life.

I know that my Savior lives, because from His glory he is continuing to do what His Father sent Him to do on earth:

> *"The Spirit of the Lord is upon Me . . . He has sent me*
> *to heal the brokenhearted . . ."*
> *Luke 4:18ac NKJ*

"He heals the brokenhearted . . ." He heals my broken heart with His Word as I read the Bible. My eternal life with God becomes more and more real to me as I get to know my heavenly Father and His beloved Son more and more intimately from the Holy Scriptures. My heavenly Father sent His Son to be the Lord of my life to save me from my sinful attitudes. It would be sinful for me to stubbornly hold on to my own limited human desires as to what I want my life or my family's life to be. Instead of this I must accept and live by His precious promises that show me what He wants to do with me and my family according to His written Word.

David's last letter and the markings in his Bible show that this is how the Lord Jesus worked in his heart, also. How wholeheartedly determined he was to obey God! This zeal did not come from some self-produced goodness in his personality. What David left behind is the account of how Jesus, the one and only Obedient Son of our heavenly Father, worked His obedience into our son's heart and life. Jesus alone is the truly Obedient One. He learned obedience to the Father by what He suffered, and He gives His Holy Spirit to those who obey Him. Jesus is the One of whom the people spoke with astonishment:

> *"Who can this be? For He commands even the winds and water, and they obey Him!" Luke 8:25c NKJ*

> *"What is this? A new teaching with authority! He commands even the unclean spirits, and they obey Him." Mark 1:27*

> *"And the multitude who were with Him when He called Lazarus out of the tomb, and raised him from the dead, were bearing Him witness.*
> *For this cause also the multitude went and met Him, because they heard that He had performed this sign.*
> *The Pharisees therefore said to one another, "You see that you are not doing any good; look, the world has gone after Him!" John 12:17-19*

Jesus Christ is the Lord of glory whom the angels worship and whose Word they obey. They do His pleasure without question. Jesus Christ is the One through whose presence in his heart our son David wrote with large letters in his last message to us:

We must obey God!
And so be blessed!
As for me and my house we will
be Baptised and serve the LORD!

David's determination overwhelms me with its unwavering resolve. Obedience to God is very costly. I had to lose our son in order to learn that I have to submit to God's plan, no matter what the cost. Jesus' death on the cross for me demands my all in return to Him. A notation in David's Bible shows that he must have understood this truth. At the Last Supper Jesus prayed,

> ". . . they are not of the world, even as I am not of the world. I do not ask Thee to take them out of the world, but to keep them from the evil one . . . Sanctify them in the truth, Thy word is truth." John 17:14a- 17

Next to this prayer David wrote,

"not happiness, but holiness"

His understanding of "happiness" is based on his resolute declaration, "We must obey God and so be blessed." To him happiness" or "blessedness," did not mean the fulfillment of his own self-pleasing dreams, but holy obedience to the Father, whereby He grants us the blessedness of seeing Him in His glory.

When David wrote, "We can have great joy in Jesus and we can bring that joy to others," he must have had a deep understanding of this truth that "joy in Jesus" comes from our Father when we obey Him with the same kind of obedience whereby our Lord Jesus went into His death by crucifixion.

My understanding of "happiness" or "blessedness" was quite incomplete when David was born. I expected it to mean that my own dreams for him would be fulfilled. At that time a friend gave me the following promise from God's Word:

> Every good and every perfect gift is from above, and comes down from the Father of lights, with whom there is no variation, or shadow of turning." James 1:17 NKJ

These words filled me with great expectation as to how God's "good gifts" would unfold in our son's life. The years passed, and he finished his graduate studies in accounting and only needed to complete his dissertation for the doctorate. It was a pleasure to watch David and Leann as they were growing in the knowledge of God and the love of His Word. David dedicated himself wholeheartedly to his responsibility as husband and father. Together, he and his family took part with great pleasure in the activities and sound Bible teaching of their church. David and Leann had a deep longing to serve the Lord as a family on the mission field. They had applied to several missions for service. I was counting on God's "good gifts" to mean that David would be used mightily in some great work for the glory of God.

Then, - like a lightning bolt - tragedy struck. David's life was cut off. In my understanding his untimely death shattered the prospect for the fruition of God's "good gifts" in his favor.

Even now, every time I pass by a cemetery, the feelings that Memory Hills Gardens evoked in me persist in my emotions. I'll never forget how the first sight of our son's simple grave crushed my heart. I stood there staring at the brass plaque with only this name engraved on it: "**DAVID DWIGHT STEERS**." A question tortured me, "Is this all that is left of my son?" The devil was hurling his arrows of despair at me. I wept bitterly,

> "Heavenly Father,
> Where are now the "good gifts" that You have promised for our son's life? What good is in a young life so suddenly cut off from all its hopes?
> How can I understand what You have done to him and to his family and to our family? Who can give me answers to my burning questions that torture me?"

Oh, the unchangeable finality of death! This is death, the curse of sin that listening to the devil's lies has brought on us. Sin! Yes, I already know this curse. I tasted it in my godless days when the displeasure of God and my guilty conscience were haunting me! My bad attitudes not only cut me off from God but also from joyful fellowship with my family. And now I have seen death! It has taken away my son from me. Oh, the hopelessness of this curse: Sin and Death!

How could I hold on to my "shield of faith" that quenches the devil's fiery darts of mistrust toward God ?

How can I hold on? I can hold on because Jesus, the "Man of sorrows," the Man who "carried all our sorrows," keeps on building me up in my faith in Him. Step by step, as I carefully search the Scriptures in order to get to know Him, He keeps on revealing Himself to me as He now is in His glory. He comforts me with answers to my questions. He has the answers!

Jesus' first disciples, too, had a shattering experience—yes, even more painful than mine—when they saw the Man of all their hopes being crucified. They saw Him dead and then buried. Jesus was the only Man who could promise them life after death, a life of eternal happiness with God, His Father. But they saw Him being condemned and executed by the official authorities as a common criminal. His tormentors delighted in adding more and more to His pain. He had to endure the most unjust and most cruel penalty ever handed down. The disciples were left without their leader to face the same hatred of the authorities as Jesus had suffered. In their despair they gathered together behind locked doors. Jesus was dead and buried. All hope was gone!

But then, even then, in spite of it all,—even after His death and burial—Jesus was able to keep His promise that He had given them before His death:

> " . . . *believe Me . . . . I will not leave you as orphans;*
> *I will come to you." John 14:1b, 18*

Jesus kept His promise! He did come back to them to heal their broken hearts. The Lord who had been crucified, who had died and who had been buried, suddenly made Himself visible to two of His forlorn disciples. He stood before them declaring that they could recognize Him from what had been written concerning Him from the beginning in the Holy Scriptures:

> *"Oh, foolish men and slow of heart to believe in all*
> *that the prophets have spoken!*
> *Was it not necessary for the Christ to suffer these*

things and to enter His glory?'
And beginning with Moses and with all the prophets,
He explained to them the things [the truth] concerning
Himself in all the Scriptures."
Luke 24:25-27

He, too, had to suffer! He, too, had to die! He came back to His disciples as their glorious, risen Lord. He showed them His wounds! He was inflicted those wounds in His anguish over the curse stamped on us. He became the Man of sorrows to take on Himself all our grief over our sin and death. When the Son of God became a human being like us, even He had to obey the Father. He obeyed the Father unto death—even the shameful death by crucifixion. He obeyed the Father to set us free from our curse of sin and death. The Father accepted His sacrifice for us and returned Him to His glory. His wounds are His love for us all. He carried His wounds on His resurrection body to His glory. We could never bear the curse of sin and death if Jesus had not come.

In my hopelessness, Jesus, my Savior, has enabled my heart to receive a miracle of new insight. The grave of my son opened my eyes to see His triumph over our curse: Sin and Death!

"He became a curse for us . . .
In order that in Christ Jesus the blessing of Abraham
might come to the Gentiles, that we might receive the
promise of the Holy Spirit through faith." Galatians
3:13a, 14

"For the law of the Spirit of life in Christ Jesus has
set you free from the law of <u>sin and death.</u>" Romans 8:2
(emphasis added)

Jesus is risen, indeed!

It is this Mighty Savior who kept His promise to come to His disciples in their despair. It is this same Jesus who had come into our David's life to teach him the joy of full obedience to His Word.

It is this Mighty Savior who made sure that he was well prepared for his unusual ministry after his homecall. David could exclaim with Jesus' first disciples:

> *"Were not our hearts burning within us while He was speaking to us on the road, while He was explaining the Scriptures to us?"*
> *Luke 24:32*

It is this same Jesus who has come to me in my despair by leading me in His Word to comforting answers to my questions. He is teaching me that He, the risen Lord of glory is now the Lord and Sovereign Ruler of every human being, even of those who are still rebellious toward Him. This understanding gives me a thankful attitude toward God in my daily circumstances and in my relationships with people. The same almighty Father of our risen Lord, who searches my heart, also searches everybody's heart. He wants everyone to know His beloved Son as their Savior from sin and death. How privileged I am that He is the Guardian of my soul and He is working in me both to will and to do the Father's good pleasure. My conscience rests in peace as I keep yielding myself to His lordship over me.

Daily God is comforting me concerning our son David. He is showing me, that our Father did keep His promise to shower our son with His "good gifts" according to His Word. Just recently I found some most touching handwritten notes left behind among David's papers:

> *"If God is*
> *Loving enough to design only good for me,*
> *Wise enough to plan what is best,*
> *Powerful enough to accomplish what*
> *His love and goodness have planned,*
>
> *How can I lack any good thing?"*
> *Vernon Berky*

Another note:

> *"Was God,*
> *Who made the universe,*
> *Any less careful,*
> *When He made me?"*

Truly our Father did shower David with the "good gift" of insights into His love and wisdom and keeping power. God did quench his thirst to know Him as his joy. But our son did not want to keep this joy to himself alone. David marked Psalm 85:6 as his prayer that all of God's people together would be granted the pleasure of being able to enjoy God:

"PRAYER"

> *"Restore us, O God of our salvation . . .*
> *Wilt Thou not Thyself revive us again, that Thy people*
> *may rejoice in Thee?"*

I add my heartfelt "Amen" and "So Be It" to this prayer. I do want to be united with the people who find their joy in God instead of wasting my time in joining the fruitless activities of the unbelievers.

How happy David must have been when in His answer God showed him the wonderful treasure He bestows on His people to make them joyful:

"PROMISE"

> *"For thus says the high and exalted One*
> *Who lives forever,*
> *Whose name is Holy,*
> *I dwell on the high and holy place,*
> *And also with the contrite and lowly of spirit*
> *In order to revive the spirit of the lowly*
> *And to revive the heart of the contrite."*
> *Isaiah 57:15*

"I . . . the high and exalted One . . . dwell . . . with the contrite and lowly of spirit . . ." David did have a lowly and humble spirit. His handwritten notes in his Bible show that he did know what it is to be contrite, to be brokenhearted over sin and to be pleading with God for a return to joyful fellowship with Him. That is why, in his last letter, he expresses so much pleasure over the gift of the Holy Spirit, through whom the high and exalted One, the risen Lord, humbled Himself to come and dwell within him, a simple, repentant, ordinary person. In his burning desire to serve God on the mission field David could have been greatly disappointed when God called him to simply continue, as a humble servant, where He has already placed him. Our loving Savior came to him to enable him to accept this humble assignment—not to some great work—but only to enjoy His mighty presence within Him. The indwelling Holy Spirit became his joy. God was pleased with David's faithfulness to His call. In his last letter to me he was able to write:

> *"We have become united with Christ. Here then is the truth:. Baptism is considered "union" in the Bible."*

The same glorious Lord who transformed the despair of His first disciples into joy, brought His joy to David so that he could write in his Bible, "We can have great joy in Jesus, and we can bring that joy to others." Our glorious Lord enabled David to bring his "joy in Jesus" to others by reaching out with compassion and respect to ordinary people, to people displeased with themselves or worried about their lives. His cheerful willingness to be helpful brought assurance to lowly people of God's love for them. Our son still has a message to bring to us. His life is not wasted! The "good gifts" of insights that God gave to David still keep on giving and multiplying for those with whom he shared them and is still sharing them.

Yes, David brought me that "joy in Jesus" from the answer he received for his prayer for joy in God. The promise of Isaiah 57:15 is one of "the good gifts" that is now multiplying in my own heart. I received the assurance that "the high and exalted One" has also condescended to come to me from His high and holy place to dwell within me. He came to revive my heart broken over my own sin and over the cruel reality and changeless finality of our son's death. He calmed my turmoil over the loss of our son by His promise that our risen Lord will raise him from death. I, a little old grandma, can enjoy my risen Lord and Savior in His written Word in the same way as His early disciples did and in the same way our son David did. The curse of sin and death would have destroyed me had God not had mercy on me.

We know that God answered David's prayer "to bring the joy of Jesus to others." The Father's promised "good gifts" still keep on giving and multiplying. What David left behind keeps on blessing me and others. We have this assurance from many friends who heard Leann's request at David's memorial service. They have answered with deeply meaningful words of what a special friend David was to them.

This past Christmas we received a greeting card from a precious Jewish young man, with whom our son became friends while he was doing graduate studies in Corpus Christi, TX from 1984 to 1987. This friend was very shy because of his features. David had a way of becoming a true and understanding friend to lonely people. After David moved on, Steve kept in touch with him by phone all through the years. On his last Christmas card Steve wrote:

> I still think of David very often and I miss him so very much. He was the kind of great friend we all hope to have at least once in our lives. He was always there for everyone.
>
> I still miss our lengthy phone calls that we shared together for many years. He knew of my heart disease and my having no vision in my left eye. He always told me: 'You don't look sick to me!' That is why I was so fond of David. He made everyone feel 'happy', <u>not sad ever</u>!
>
> Love Steve"
>
> (underline by Steve)

His parents could tell whenever Steve had been talking with David. He came into their room beaming with a happy smile, and they would exclaim, "We know what you've been doing! You've been talking with David!" Yes, David did bring the joy of Jesus to others.

To me he is also bringing further joy with a new insight that I now have concerning my role in my family. In his last letter he shared his happy excitement over God's blessing on any family even if there is only one believer in it. What David wrote touched me deeply,

"By just one person becoming a believer brought a blessing on everyone in the household, including the unbelievers and the children.
"WOW! All are blessed -
(1 Corinthians 7:14) -
This goes back to God's promise to
Abraham in Genesis 12:3."

David treasured this everlasting promise of God to Abraham that in him every family on earth will be blessed. I can know that even now, with David gone, God's blessing is on his family and on our whole family and on every family who hears and obeys His Word. God fulfilled His promise when He sent His Son to earth, as it is written:

> *"You are sons of the prophets, and of the covenant which God made with our fathers, saying to Abraham, 'And in your seed all the families of the earth shall be blessed.'*
> *To you, first, God having raised up His Servant Jesus, sent Him to bless you, in turning away every one of you from your iniquities."*
> *Acts 3:25. 26 NKJ*

Jesus blesses us by saving each one of us from our sin. David was happy that by his faith in God and through his wholehearted obedience to His Word he would secure His blessing on his family. For the sake of my family I, too, now keep my heart open for "the blessing of Abraham," the gift of the Holy Spirit, so that He can use me for my loved ones' blessing. I trust God for His enabling grace to make me obedient to His Word so I can have the joy of Jesus in me. Whenever I fail I immediately confess this to Him. Then He takes pleasure in releasing me from guilt and to take me back into His loving arms. My joyful attitude is the proof to my family that it is truly a pleasure to have God in charge of my life. I can't bless my family if I complain against what God has done. Before I can expect anyone else to obey, I have to obey first:

> *"Behold, to obey is better than sacrifice . . .*
> *For rebellion is as the sin of witchcraft."*
> *1 Samuel 15:22, 23a*

David's last letter brings peace into my heart as I ponder the future that is waiting for his precious orphaned children and all our family's children in this terribly evil and dangerous world. The only safety for them is to know God's great, individual plan for each of their lives and to obey that plan. As God is working obedience through His Holy Spirit in my own heart, I know that He is faith- fully doing the same in my children's and grandchildren's hearts, too. He is leading them, also, into experiences whereby, the Father in His great wisdom makes Himself known to them according to their own needs. God alone has the power to change the human heart, even my own. Before I knew God's Word, I imagined that I could—by my own shortsighted human efforts—bring about changes in my husband's or my children's attitudes. Now I know that my part is to live according to the Good News of our Lord Jesus that it is He who saves us from sin.

In my prayers for my children and grandchildren I receive a new resolve from David's example to take God's promises to heart like he did. From his notations in his Bible it is evident that he did more than pray for his children. He searched God's Word until he received the assurance that God did hear and answer his prayers. It is our Father who gave him this "good gift" of confidence in His Word. I have learned that God is most pleased with my prayers when I take to heart His promises like David did and add my own

"Amen" and "So Be It" to them. It is so wonderful to know that my heavenly Father is pleased when I cast my worries on Him in prayer because then He takes the proper action. He is not pleased when I rely on my own efforts to force results. I receive new confidence as I join David's prayer for all our children. He addressed his prayer to the Almighty Father to whom all our forefathers in the faith had prayed:

"PRAYER"

"O Lord, the God of our fathers, art Thou not God in the heavens? And art Thou not ruler over all the kingdoms of the nations?
Power and might are in Thy hand so that no one can stand against Thee. . . .
. . . we . . . stand before this house and before Thee (for Thy name is in this house) and cry to Thee in our distress, and Thou wilt hear and deliver us." 2 Chronicles 20:6-9

This is the Mighty God, the God of Abraham, who then led David to His answer, assuring him of His blessing on his children:

"PROMISE"

"And I will establish My covenant between Me and you and your descendants after you throughout their generations for an everlasting covenant, to be God to you and to your descendants after you." Genesis 17:7

David recognized the fulfillment of this Old Testament promise in the New Testament, the good news of Pentecost that he kept repeating to me in his last letter:

"Mom, remember from Acts 2:39: "For the promise is to you and to <u>your children</u>."
(underline by David)

"We are counted into union with Christ!"
(Romans 6:5 in David's words)

This blessing, the blessing of Abraham, the promise of the Holy Spirit to him and to his children was burning in David's heart as he was writing his last letter to me. This promise is still resting on David's loved ones, on Leann, Christalyn, Benjamin and Solomon Isaac. From this promise David received the unshakeable assurance that the God of Abraham, the God of all of His people throughout all their generations, would be the God of his family forever. Yes, I continually remember and claim with David the promise of the Holy Spirit's work in the hearts of his children and all the children in our family. More than ever I cling to the truth of these precious words:

> *"And if you belong to Christ, then you are Abraham's seed, and heirs according to the promise." Galatians 3:29*

My husband and I have been able to visit Leann and the children quite often. The Lord keeps assuring us that He is very present in their little home and in their midst. The other day Phil overheard Benjamin saying to his mother, "I wish Daddy was here!" Leann took him into her arms and said, "I wish that, too! But, remember, God is our Father now!"

I keep thanking our almighty Father for His work in Leann. We know that He is the One who is teaching her such wholehearted dependence on Him. He has given her a loving, sensitive heart toward the needs of others. Instead of feeling sorry for herself she finds ways of being helpful to other single mothers, helping them with their children. This way she is teaching her own children, too, to love others rather than concentrating on their own loss. I recall what Leann said at David's funeral, "Now I have to walk the talk, rather than just talk the walk."

Our Lord is faithful to His promise:

> *" I will not leave you as orphans; I will come to you..." John 14:18*

Recently Leann sent us the following letter which shows that truly God is keeping the promises He made to David for his family:

> As I look back, I marvel at the faithfulness of God. I have remarked to several friends more than once that God tailors His fatherhood to my kids. He is not just a "general Father in the sky, sort of being," but He acts as a true Father in meeting the needs and desires of my children..
>
> Of course, we all long for Him in the flesh to touch and to hold. But for now, we have to be satisfied to hold and touch Him in His written Word..

With Leann we have good reason to join the Psalmist in a praise to God that we have discovered after David's death:

> *"Sing to God, sing praises to His name . . .*
> *"Father of the fatherless," and "Defender of widows," is*
> *God in His holy habitation . . ."*
> *(Psalm 68:5 NKJ with my own spelling and punctuation)*

So is our God in "His holy habitation!" With Leann and the children we know that the loving daddy of their family is there now singing praises and watching our Father, who through His beloved Son, is faithfully carrying out the promises He made to him concerning his loved ones.

Now that David is in "God's holy habitation" I notice so much more fervently what our Bible says about God's people who already live there with Him. They already see the face of the One to whom David prayed for an obedient heart:

"PRAYER"

> *"I shall keep Thy statutes; Do not forsake me utterly."*
> *Psalm 119:8*

"PROMISE"

*"Now to Him who is able to keep you from stumbling,
and to make you stand in the presence of His glory blameless with (exceeding NKJ) great joy, to the only God our
Savior, (who alone is wise NKJ) through Jesus Christ our
Lord, be glory, majesty, dominion and authority, before all
time and now and forever. Amen." Jude 24, 25*

This wonderful promise is now a reality to our son, David. And
this is the awesome magnitude of God's purpose for my life:

"to keep me from stumbling and to make me stand in
the presence of His glory blameless with exceeding
great joy . . . "

This is God's great plan not for me only, but for all His own, who
were born again into His family by faith in the death and resurrection of His beloved Son. We who pray to the Father in Jesus' name,
we all are the family of the same God. Our God is the Father of our
Lord Jesus Christ, the God of the Holy Scriptures, the God of
Abraham, the God of Isaac, the God of Jacob, the God of Moses, the
God of king David, the God of all the prophets and all the apostles.

David's grave constantly reminds me of the temporality of our
life here on earth. This same insight was the guiding principle of
Abraham's life. In Hebrews 11:9 we read that he could have built a
city in the land where God had led him and which He promised to
give to him forever. But instead of building a city Abraham lived in
tents with his sons because his heart was fixed on the heavenly
Jerusalem, the city of the living God, that God Himself is building,
where He Himself lives with His people. Abraham and his sons
confessed that,

" . . . *they were strangers and exiles on the earth . . .
they desired a better country, that is a heavenly one.
Therefore God is not ashamed to be called their God; for
He has prepared a city for them." Hebrews 11:13c, 16*

God honored Abraham's faith by calling Himself "The God of Abraham." I know that "The God of Abraham" is also "The God of Maria Vágó Steers," because my heart, also, is fixed on that Holy City where Jesus is preparing a place for me in His Father's house. It is from there that Jesus is coming back, bringing our loved ones with Him.

I am so thankful that the heavenly Father gave me Jesus, His Son, to be my Savior from sin. He is our risen Lord who is transforming me into His likeness by His resurrection power. From His glory He is exerting His authority over my heart, making me, a stubborn, self-centered person into a loving, obedient child of the heavenly Father. Now I know that which in my sinful state I could not know. I know that our God is worthy of my obedience no matter what the cost. I love to praise God with king David:

"Oh Lord, how I love Your law!
It is my meditation all the day.
You, through Your commandments,
make me wiser than my enemies;
For they are ever with me . . .
I have restrained my feet from every evil way,
that I may keep Your word.
For You Yourself have taught me."
Selected from *Psalm 119:97- 102 NKJ,* emphasis added

Our son David did not die but went to live with Jesus in the heavenly Jerusalem, according to Jesus' prayer:

"Father, I will that all those whom You have given Me
be with Me where I am, that they may see My glory, the
glory which You have given Me - in your great love to Me
- before the foundation of the world." John 17:24 NASV

Our God is a miracle-working God. I know this because of what He is doing in my heart through the testimony that David left behind. God was the joy of his heart and life. This made him a pleasure to God and God is speaking His approval of David's life to me.

God is using our son—even though he has gone home to be with the Lord—to be still speaking to me, exhorting me to make our God the joy of my heart. David is still spreading the good news of the greatness of our God, the God of the Holy Bible. Our God is able to do above all that we can ask or think.

Our Father is abundant in wisdom and loving kindness, in tender mercies and forgiveness and generosity toward all those who call on Him in Jesus' name.

From Psalm 78:72 He is assuring me that I can depend on Jesus, our Great Shepherd to faithfully lead us, His flock, with the integrity of His heart and the skillfulness of His hands. All glory belongs to Him! Those who call on His holy name will never be disappointed.

Even when at times tears well up, I still can say, truly, Jesus heals the brokenhearted! And at the same time also wells up a fervent prayer in my heart:

Our heavenly Father,

May our perfectly obedient Lord and Savior Jesus Christ by the precious blood of His new covenant with us, through His Holy Spirit bring about wholehearted obedience to Your Word in the hearts of David's beloved children, Christalyn, Benjamin, and Solomon Isaac. This I pray for all of us, David's whole family, and for all Your own children in Your great family.

May You, our Almighty Father, cause to blossom forth to full fruition Your promised "good gifts" on David's life. May You fulfill the desire of David's heart by using his testimony that he left behind:

"We can have great joy in Jesus, and we can bring that joy to others."

Father, You reward with joy all those who obey You with their whole heart. This is the joy of Jesus, Your beloved Son, who in obedience to You, loved us so much that He gave Himself on the cross for us.

Father, I join my prayer to David's prayer, the prayer that he prayed with the Psalmist:

> *"Restore us, O God of our salvation . . .*
> *Wilt Thou not Thyself revive us again, that Thy people*
> *may rejoice in Thee?" Psalm 85:6*

Father, I ask You, teach us to find our joy in Jesus! I ask You in His holy name, Amen."

With a thankful and eternally praising heart

David's mother, Grandma Steers,
Maria Vágó Steers
Mrs. Philip L Steers, Jr

Printed in the United States
118349LV00003B/208-330/A